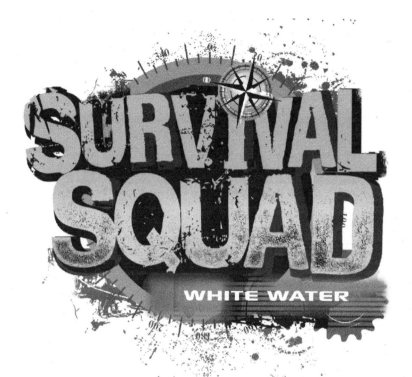

SURVIVAL SQUAD

WHITE WATER

JONATHAN ROCK

RED FOX

With thanks to Paul May

SURVIVAL SQUAD: WHITE WATER
A RED FOX BOOK 978 1 862 30968 5

First published in Great Britain by Red Fox,
an imprint of Random House Children's Publishers UK
A Random House Group Company

This edition published 2013

1 3 5 7 9 10 8 6 4 2

Set in 13/19 pt Goudy by Falcon Oast Graphic Art Ltd.

Red Fox Books are published by Random House Children's Publishers UK,
61–63 Uxbridge Road, London W5 5SA

www.**randomhousechildrens**.co.uk
www.**totallyrandombooks**.co.uk
www.**randomhouse**.co.uk

Addresses for companies within The Random House Group Limited can be found
at: www.randomhouse.co.uk/offices.htm

THE RANDOM HOUSE GROUP Limited Reg. No. 954009

A CIP catalogue record for this book is available from the British Library.

Printed and bound in Great Britain by
CPI Group (UK) Ltd, Croydon, CR0 4YY

CHAPTER 1

A lone kayaker paddled swiftly down a turbulent river. Brown water foamed white where it was forced between giant rocks, and its tremendous power hurled the tiny yellow kayak about like a toy, threatening to obliterate the paddler. His blue helmet frequently disappeared beneath the churning currents, but he never once stopped paddling.

'How cool is that?' exclaimed Priya, her dark brown eyes glued to the screen. 'Is that really what we're going to be doing?'

Julie, Assistant Scout Leader of the 6th Matfield Scout Troop, hit the PAUSE button on her laptop, and the image on the screen froze. A wide smile split Julie's suntanned face and her eyes sparkled. 'I do hope not,' she said with a laugh. 'I know you think you're ready for

1

anything, Priya, but this is a big river in spate and you're watching an experienced kayaker there.'

Sitting with Priya were the other members of Tiger Patrol. In two weeks' time they would be setting off for their summer camp in the north, and kayaking was going to be a big part of the trip. Connor Sutcliff, the Tigers' Patrol Leader, had been watching the video with intense concentration in his blue eyes. He was almost sure he recognized the kayaker . . .

Rick, their Scout Leader, was standing with Julie. He was tall and muscular, with a weather-beaten face and close-cropped grey hair. He glanced at the frozen image. 'Go on then,' he said to Julie. 'You'd better show them the rest of it.'

On the screen the kayaker spun into action. Suddenly the little boat was facing the wrong way. It was flung onto its side by the power of the water, and then the whole screen was filled with swirling foam.

'Awesome!' breathed Andy Mackenzie, a tall boy with longish brown hair who was sitting behind Priya. 'That's been filmed with a helmet

2

cam. This is incredible footage!'

Andy was a passionate photographer and moviemaker and he had filmed many of Tiger Patrol's exploits during the past year.

'Maybe you could get a camera like that and film us,' suggested Abby, Andy's best friend and neighbour. A strand of her long hair had escaped from her ponytail and she pushed it back behind her ear. 'That would be so cool.'

'I can't afford it,' Andy replied. 'I only wish I could! Hey, look at that!'

Now they were seeing the view from another camera, positioned high above the raging river. The camera zoomed out and panned round to the right.

'No!' gasped the small dark-haired boy beside Connor. 'I don't believe it! They must be crazy!'

Toby was the Tigers' Assistant Patrol Leader. Toby threw himself into almost every activity with enthusiasm and determination, but Connor knew that he hadn't really enjoyed their first experience of kayaking in the local swimming pool, although he had worked as hard as any of them.

The camera now showed a massive waterfall. Across the whole width of the river, water was thundering down into a seething rocky cauldron of spray, foam and tumbled water. Even through the small loudspeakers attached to Julie's computer, the noise sounded tremendous. The kayaker was about fifty metres from the waterfall now, paddling hard. Suddenly the view changed, and they were looking through the helmet camera again, seeing what he was seeing.

'Oh, wow!' exclaimed Priya, eyes shining. 'He's really going to do it!'

The kayak flipped over the edge and the camera was blotted out by white spray. The film cut back to the view from the bank and they saw the kayak plunge vertically into the maelstrom below. Connor held his breath, and he realized that the others were doing the same. There was another cut to the kayaker's point of view, and they were looking at rushing water, the flash of a paddle, spinning silhouettes of dark pine trees. Then, from above, they saw the bottom of an upturned kayak, the blade of a paddle digging into the rushing torrent – and miraculously the kayak was upright again and heading off downstream as the paddler somehow found time to punch the air in triumph.

The assembled Scouts let out a cheer, and Connor could contain himself no longer. 'It's you, Rick, isn't it?' he said. 'I saw your face, just for a second.'

Rick laughed. 'Well spotted,' he said. 'I thought my face was under water most of the time. It certainly felt like it!'

'And can *we* do something like that?' demanded Priya. 'I mean, not kayak over a waterfall, but will we be paddling on white water?'

Rick smiled at her. 'We'll see how you get on,' he said. 'After last week's session at the pool, I think we might have to concentrate on teaching you all to paddle in a straight line first.'

There was some laughter at this, but Connor noticed a few embarrassed-looking faces as he glanced around at the rest of the Troop.

'You don't need to worry,' Rick told them. 'Don't forget that you have excellent kayak instructors.'

The Scouts laughed. Rick and Julie were the instructors in question, and Connor knew that they really were very good.

'Believe it or not, I was terrified of water when I first got into a kayak,' Rick continued. 'So there's hope for you all. By the time our camp is over you'll all be old hands, but remember, this camp isn't just about kayaking. We'll be hill walking on one of the days, and gorge-walking on another, so there'll be plenty of variety. Now, off you go and change into your scruffs. I'm hoping that most of you will get your Survival Skills Badge on this trip. If you can't even cook with a frying pan, you'll find it very tricky cooking over an open fire with no utensils, so we'll make sure you can all fry sausages and eggs at least!'

'I don't know how Rick could do that,' said Toby as he and Jay tended the Tigers' fire in the altar that was set up on the patch of grass behind Scout HQ. 'It looked seriously scary. And he was right: I *still* can't paddle in a straight line!'

'You'll soon learn,' said Jay. He had joined the Scouts just a year ago, at the same time as Priya, and although he had been a reluctant Scout at first, he had soon become firm friends with Toby. 'You're getting good at falling in anyway,' he added, laughing.

'Ha, ha,' muttered Toby gloomily. 'I sink. That's what worries me.'

'It's 'cos you're so thin,' Jay told him. 'But you do float really, or you would if you didn't keep fighting the water all the time. I've never seen anyone splash as much as you do.'

'You'll be wearing a buoyancy aid,' said Priya, appearing beside them with a pack of sausages and a box of eggs. 'You heard what Rick said. They wouldn't be taking us kayaking if we couldn't do it.'

'That's just it,' Toby replied. 'I don't want to mess up. Part of the camp is going to be a three-day expedition in kayaks, and if I can't improve, then they might not let me go.'

'You'll be fine. Tell him, Abby.'

'Of course you will,' said Abby, placing the

frying pan on the grille and pouring in a little oil. As she looked up at Toby, her hand slipped, and some of the oil slopped over the side of the pan. There was a brief flicker of flame before Abby removed the pan from the heat.

'Hey, Survival Squad,' called Sajiv, the Panthers' Patrol Leader, 'don't set yourselves on fire!'

'At least we've got a fire,' retorted Abby. 'All *you've* got is smoke!' She was looking at the Panthers' fire, which had nearly gone out. 'Serves them right,' she went on. 'I wish we'd never been given that stupid nickname. They all love it when we get something wrong.'

'No, they don't,' said Connor reasonably. 'They love winding you up, Abby, that's all.'

'Because it's so easy,' added Andy.

'But you can see why they might be jealous,' said Priya. 'We do seem to have more excitement than anyone else.'

'Lost in the mist,' said Jay.

'Stuck on a cliff . . .'

'Riding in a helicopter . . .'

'Catching rustlers . . .'

They were all talking at once as they remembered the incredible adventures they'd had in the course of the year. 'We weren't actually lost,' said Toby.

'It just felt like it,' replied Priya, remembering how scared she'd been on her first expedition.

'How about we just ensure that we don't make any more mistakes,' Connor said, laughing. 'Like letting our *own* fire go out, for instance!'

Abby spun round again with a cry, only to see the sausages sizzling happily over a perfect fire. She looked back and found the other five Tigers grinning broadly at her.

'I told you,' laughed Andy. 'Winding you up is just too easy. I think it's time to add the eggs. I'm starving!'

Two weeks later the Tigers were eating again, but now the smell of pine woods was all around them, and a river rushed past not ten metres from the grassy platform where they had pitched their tents. Between the trees Connor could see the blue outlines of distant mountains. Their summer camp had begun.

'My mouth is on fire,' said Andy as the Tigers sat on an old tree trunk beside the river. He spoke loudly and Connor saw the white cable of his iPod headphones snaking up under his long brown hair as his head nodded in time to the music.

'I know,' agreed Toby, taking a swig from his water bottle. 'That was the hottest chilli I've ever eaten.'

'Hot?' Priya looked astonished. She also looked incredibly cool, even though she claimed the cargo pants and T-shirt were her oldest, scruffiest clothes. 'You're kidding, right?' she continued. 'I wish I'd brought a bottle of chilli sauce with me. You haven't got one in your bag, have you, Toby?'

Toby's enormous rucksack was legendary. It often contained the most surprising things and was always incredibly heavy. 'No,' he replied. 'But I wish I'd packed a fire extinguisher for my mouth! I can't believe you don't think it's hot.'

The 6th Matfield were sharing the campsite

with several other Scout Troops. They had arrived a few hours earlier after a long, stuffy journey in three minibuses, all heavily loaded with camping equipment and towing trailers loaded with kayaks. As well as Rick and Julie they had several other helpers with them. There were two Explorer Scouts, Martina and Gary, as well as Connor's dad and Usha, a rock-climbing friend of Julie's who had driven the minibus the Tigers had travelled in.

The campsite extended through a series of clearings in the trees, and the Tigers had all agreed that their own spot was easily the best: it was right beside the river.

'Why don't we explore along the bank?' Toby suggested. 'It might take our minds off the pain.'

'You're all so sad,' scoffed Priya. 'I'll get my parents to invite you round for a meal. After you've eaten my mum's food you'll never think anything is hot ever again!'

They got to their feet, but as they set off along the path, they saw a group of kayakers speeding along the river towards them, paddles flashing.

'They're Sea Scouts,' said Toby, who had spotted the logo on the kayaks.

'They can certainly handle those kayaks,' said Connor admiringly.

The Tigers stopped and watched as the Sea Scouts brought their kayaks expertly up to the bank and helped each other to climb out.

'Can we give you a hand?' Connor offered as they started to haul their boats out of the water.

'No, thanks, we're cool.' The boy who spoke seemed to be the leader. He crouched by his boat and lifted it easily. Moments later all ten boats were on the bank. 'We're the Otter Patrol and some of the Seals,' the boy said, removing his helmet to reveal dark, very wet hair. 'We're from the Welland Bay Sea Scouts. I'm Max.'

Connor introduced himself and the other Tigers. Toby saw the Sea Scouts glancing at the Matfield kayaks, and suddenly he found himself viewing them through an outsider's eyes. He had to admit, they did look very old and battered.

'So where are you going?' Max asked.

'We have to do some more training,' Abby

told him, casting an envious glance at the kayaks behind him. 'Then we're going on an expedition downriver. We'll be camping for two nights on the way. It's the first time we've done anything like this in kayaks.'

'Really?' A slim Scout removed her helmet and shook water out of her fair hair. 'You'll have a great time. There's nothing better than kayaking. We came for the white water upstream. Are those yours?'

'Yes,' said Abby, a little defensively. 'They're a bit old, but they've been on lots of expeditions.'

'You're right,' said the girl, flashing them a smile. 'They're cool. See you around maybe.'

With that, the Sea Scouts picked up their gleaming kayaks in a well-drilled routine and headed off across the grass, leaving the Tigers staring after them.

'She thought it was tame, what we'll be doing,' said Abby. 'She was too polite to say, but you could see it in her eyes.'

'I don't think so,' said Connor, watching the girl disappear between the trees. 'I thought she was OK. And we don't have to worry about a thing. Whatever Rick and Julie have planned for us, it definitely won't be tame. You all saw Rick in that kayak. He loves excitement. And I'm absolutely certain that's what we're going to get!'

CHAPTER 2

Abby was still thinking about the Sea Scouts' comments early the next morning as she made French toast for the whole troop in the kitchen tent. The Tigers had been busy since six o'clock, lighting the fires, preparing the bread and eggs and setting the tables. 'That girl didn't know what she was talking about,' Abby muttered as she flipped a slice over in the pan. 'As if we'd ever have a tame expedition!'

'Well, we won't, will we?' Andy was operating the frying pan next to hers, nodding his head in time to the music on his iPod. 'Something unexpected will happen and we'll end up having an adventure. We always do.'

'I want to kayak on white water like them. We're going to a lake today. It'll be just like kayaking in a swimming pool.'

Andy laughed. 'I bet you didn't sleep properly,' he said. 'That's why you're so grumpy. You're always like that after the first night in a tent.'

'Five minutes, Tigers,' warned Rick, passing through the kitchen to inspect their preparations. 'You haven't got the milk out yet, Connor. And, Andy, take out those headphones. Concentrate on your cooking.'

Andy put the headphones in his pocket. 'I cook better with music,' he told Abby.

'I suppose that's why you're burning the French toast,' Abby replied innocently – whereupon he gave a yelp and turned back to his pan.

Connor quickly checked on the other preparations. Toby and Priya were in charge of the drinks. Jay was sorting out the plates and bowls. It all seemed OK. He hurried down to the river, where they had stored the large plastic bottles of milk in a net. The water was cold, and Connor knew that it had started out in the distant mountains that they'd glimpsed the previous evening. He felt the sun on his back. It was going to be another hot day. It was a shame they had to get in the minibuses and drive to the lake. The river looked shady and inviting.

'Connor!' Toby's voice interrupted his thoughts. 'Hurry up! It's time!'

Connor rushed back to the kitchen area with the milk as a horde of hungry Scouts descended. They demolished all the food that the Tigers had prepared in an astonishingly short time, burned bits included.

'I'm glad that's over,' said Abby, nibbling her last bit of eggy bread as the other Scouts left the eating area. 'It's hard work, cooking for all those people.'

'You know you enjoyed it really,' Connor told her. 'Me and Toby will wash up. You and Andy wipe down the surfaces and dry, and Jay and Priya can put away.'

'You'd better hurry,' said Connor's dad, walking past with a large bag of equipment.

Chris Sutcliff was a GP in Matfield, but he spent a lot of his spare time helping out with the Scouts. The Tigers all knew that, like Connor's grandpa, Chris had succeeded in becoming a

Queen's Scout. They also knew that Connor hoped to follow in their footsteps one day.

'Nice breakfast!' Chris said with a smile. 'We're leaving in half an hour.'

The minibuses turned off the main road, heading down a narrow, bumpy forest track towards the lake, and finally emerging in a clearing. A wide stretch of dark water glittered in the sunshine, surrounded on all sides by pine forest.

'This is the perfect place to learn about raft-building,' Rick told the Scouts when they had gathered by the water's edge. 'You've got a pile of logs each, and plenty of rope. First you build your raft, then we have a race.'

'I thought we were going kayaking,' said Abby. 'I mean, why do we need to build rafts?'

'It'll be fun,' Rick said. 'It's a great chance to put your knots and lashings to practical use. Rafts may look clumsy but in rough water they're more stable than canoes – though they can be hard to steer, as you'll probably find out.'

'You couldn't go very far in one, though, could

you?' asked Kerry, the Kestrels' Patrol Leader.

'Well, we hope you'll manage to get to the other side of the lake at least,' replied Julie. 'People have travelled enormous distances on rafts. Haven't you heard of the Kon-Tiki expedition?'

'Of course!' exclaimed Toby. 'They made a raft out of balsa-wood logs to prove that people could have sailed from South America across the Pacific Ocean to Polynesia. And they did it too. It was a man called Thor Heyerdahl in nineteen forty-seven—' He came to a sudden stop. All the Scouts were staring at him.

'How do you know all this stuff?' asked Sajiv. 'You should go on one of those TV shows and win loads of money.'

They all laughed. 'Toby's right as usual,' said Julie, smiling. 'But for today we'll just try to make rafts that don't sink. We'll use a very simple construction method, lashing six or seven big logs to cross-pieces. Each Patrol can split into two teams, and there's an instruction sheet for each team. You have an hour and a half – then the race will begin, whether you're ready or not!'

Connor took the laminated sheets of instructions from Julie. 'It looks simple enough,' he said as Tiger Patrol headed towards the piles of logs. 'Andy and Abby, you can be together, and you can have Toby to make sure you get your lashings right.'

'What are you saying?' demanded Abby, who was famous for rushing into every situation without always thinking first. Then she grinned. 'Yeah, OK. I'll try to be careful. Ready, Andy? Let's get started.'

Connor led Priya and Jay over to their pile of logs. 'We can build it here,' he told them. 'We lay two logs on the ground and then lash the others onto them crosswise, one piece of rope for each side.'

Jay was inspecting the logs. 'They're kind of big,' he said. 'Take the other end, Priya. Let's see how heavy they are.'

The two of them picked up the log and then put it back on the ground. 'I thought so,' said Jay. 'It's easy enough to lift them one at a time, but we'll never lift the whole raft. We should build it in the water.'

Connor crouched down and raised one end of the log. 'Good thinking, Jay. Imagine if we'd had to undo it all!'

'We'd better tell the others,' said Priya. A hundred metres away, Andy and Toby were shifting logs into position and Abby had already started lashing them together. Priya waved and shouted, but she just waved back and carried on.

'Run and tell them,' said Connor. 'Me and Jay will start carrying these to the water . . .'

'Abby was annoyed,' Priya reported when she returned a few moments later. 'She'd already lashed two logs together. I think we'll probably finish before them at this rate.'

'I don't mind who finishes first,' Connor said. 'The main thing is to make sure our lashings don't come undone.' He started manoeuvring the logs into position in the shallow water as ripples lapped at his bare legs. 'Hey, it's nice and cool in here. Bring the rope, Jay – let's get started.'

* * *

A short distance away along the shore of the lake, Andy and Toby had moved all their logs into place. Now Toby was tying a clove hitch round the first of the cross-pieces. He pulled it tight. 'OK, now it goes around twice under there and crosses over, see? Then we pull it tight, make a half-hitch on this connector log, and we're ready to move on to number two.'

'Are you saying I wasn't doing it properly before? Here, let me do the next one.' Abby pushed Toby aside and set to work.

Toby watched as she looped the rope neatly under the next big log and then started to make a square lashing. 'OK,' he said, consulting the instructions, 'now take a frapping turn and pull it tight. You can just do a half-hitch around the connector and then we can start on the next one. Cool – that's perfect!'

Abby stood up and stretched. 'Shall I take over?' Toby asked.

'No way! I'm enjoying this. I'm going to show you I can do it all myself.'

Andy paddled out of the water and took out

his camcorder. 'I can film you doing it,' he said. 'It'll be the latest in my series of "How To" videos.'

Toby helped Abby to get all seven logs into position and she finished off the final one with a neat clove-hitch. 'There,' she said proudly. 'What do you think?'

'Excellent.' Toby nodded. 'I couldn't have done it better.'

Abby beamed and swept back the hair that had escaped from her ponytail. 'Now I'm going to do the other connector,' she said. 'Come on, Andy, you must have got enough footage now. Give Toby a break.'

Andy put his camera away and stepped into the water. Toby glanced at his watch. They had plenty of time. There were some experienced-looking kayakers out on the water and he walked a short distance along the bank to take a closer look. If he could only make turns like that! he thought wistfully. If he could only paddle in a straight line . . .

He was soon absorbed in watching, and was

astonished when he heard Rick calling, 'Time's up, everyone! You've got five minutes to get ready. When I blow my whistle, the race will begin.'

Toby ran back to the others. 'Have you finished?' he asked Abby. 'I'm sorry, I should have been helping.'

'No need,' Abby grunted. 'Just this last log, and we're done. We stopped for a while so Andy could get some footage of how to tie the knots,' she explained. 'It slowed us down a bit, but we've finished now. Just in time!'

She stood up, her freckled face flushed and triumphant. The completed raft floated in the water, and Toby felt relief wash over him.

'Look,' said Andy, pointing his camera along the shore. 'The others are test-driving theirs. Awesome!'

The raft was coming towards them. Priya was sitting in the middle while Connor and Jay, both lying down, were laughing as they paddled it along with their hands.

'Great,' said Connor when they drew alongside. 'You've finished too. You'd better get your buoyancy aids on, though, and grab some paddles. I think Rick's about to blow his whistle.'

Rick signalled for them all to get ready, and Connor, Jay and Priya pushed their raft carefully out through the shallow water. Connor was glad that they had finished so quickly. It had given them time to work out the best arrangement for paddling. Priya took up position in the middle while Connor and Jay steadied the logs.

'I reckon you'd have to make one quite a lot bigger than this if you wanted to carry anything really heavy,' Jay said, looking at the water splashing up through the gap. 'You'd need bigger logs, and more of them.'

'I've seen them with barrels tied on,' Priya said. 'That would help, wouldn't it?'

Jay grunted agreement as he and Connor pulled themselves onto opposite sides of the raft. The logs tilted alarmingly for a second, but Priya quickly shifted her weight and the raft floated level again. She handed the kayak paddles to the two boys and they began to power the raft out onto the lake. Connor glanced to his right and saw that the others had copied their arrangement, with Toby, the smallest, sitting in the centre, while Andy and Abby paddled.

Rick let out a piercing blast on his whistle, and the air filled with excited yells as the Scouts attempted to direct their rafts towards the middle of the lake. Connor concentrated on trying to match his strokes with Jay's, but the raft was incredibly hard to control, and as they moved out from the shelter of the trees, the wind caught it and began pushing it back towards the shore. Connor and Jay paddled as hard as they could but the raft just spun round and continued to drift.

'We're going to end up back where we started,' said Priya, who seemed to be enjoying herself. All the rafts had been launched now, and she noticed that most of the paddlers were having the same trouble as Connor and Jay. 'Hey, look – there are Abby and Andy and Toby. They're going straighter than anyone. Toby's got his paddle at the back. I see what he's doing!' she cried. 'He's using it to steer.'

'And Abby's paddling from the front,' said Jay. 'It makes sense. 'Toby's paddle is a sort of rudder. Why don't we try that?'

It was a complicated business, rearranging themselves on the raft, and they nearly tipped it over before they managed it, but as soon as Connor plunged his paddle into the water behind the raft, they began to move forward in a more or less straight line.

'Nice one, Toby,' Connor yelled across the water. Then: 'Oh no! What's happening to them?'

'It's their raft,' said Priya. 'I think it's coming apart!'

Abby, Andy and Toby were all shouting at once, frantically trying to keep the logs together. It was no good. Seconds later they were all in the water, clinging to the ruins of their raft. On every other raft the Scouts were helpless with laughter, and they let their rafts drift to a standstill while the watched the floundering Tigers. Even Rick and Julie, who were supervising from their kayaks, couldn't hide their smiles as they raced to the rescue.

'Quick,' urged Connor quietly. 'Keep paddling, Jay. While they're all busy watching!'

'Oh, yes,' Priya hissed. 'Go on, Jay, paddle! They haven't realized yet. We can win!'

Suddenly they heard cries of dismay and panic behind them. Connor laughed as he glanced back to see the other teams in complete disarray, desperately trying to set their rafts in motion again. He heard Abby, Andy and Toby yelling encouragement as they steered their raft calmly to the far side of the lake and beached it in the shallows. Connor, Jay and Priya all stood up with their arms aloft, then glanced at each other before running into the deliciously cool water, where they jumped up and down, punching the air in celebration.

CHAPTER 3

Lunch was over, and the Tigers were lined up in their kayaks in the middle of the lake. Toby was still feeling guilty about their shipwreck in the raft. He really should have checked Abby's lashings. She'd obviously rushed the job, and she definitely hadn't tied a proper knot at the end. He had watched, horrified, as the logs slowly moved apart, depositing him and Andy and Abby in the water. Even so, they had all managed to laugh about it, especially when Connor and the others had won the race.

The wind was tugging at Toby's kayak, trying to twist it round, and he struggled to keep it facing forward. He could see that the others were having the same trouble, and yet ahead of them, Julie was managing to keep her kayak effortlessly in position. It was very different from paddling in a swimming pool.

'OK, everyone,' Julie called. 'Paddle towards me. Don't look down – look up and forwards.'

Toby gritted his teeth and tried to concentrate on where he was trying to go, but the kayak didn't seem to want to go that way. He was spinning back to face the shore. He dug his paddle into the water to try to stop the spin and found himself lurching horribly in the other direction. For a moment he thought he was going into the water; then he felt the boat stabilize miraculously, and Julie came up alongside him, hand on his kayak.

'Relax,' she said with a smile. 'Paddle gently and sit forward . . . That's it!'

'Your face, Toby!' said Priya as he finally rejoined the rest of the group. 'Did you know you were sticking your tongue out? You need to watch out you don't bite it off.'

Toby watched enviously as she paddled round in a neat circle and came back to join him. She seemed to be a natural at kayaking. 'This is fun.

I've been looking forward to it ever since I joined the Scouts!' she said, her dark eyes shining.

Julie instructed them to choose a landmark on the shore and try to steer in a straight line towards it. Toby concentrated on keeping his strokes even, placing the paddle in the water by his toes and bringing it out fast when it reached his hip. The trouble was, he could only do one thing at a time. When he focused on the tip of the paddle and how it entered the water, he lost sight of the tall tree he was aiming for, and soon found himself turning in circles again. 'I'll never get the hang of this,' he told Jay, who had paddled over to see how he was doing.

'You're trying too hard. Remember what Julie said about shallow correction strokes? When you go off line, you're digging the paddle in too far.'

'I'm doing my best.'

'You'll get it in the end,' laughed Jay. 'I'm a lot better already. Watch!'

He sprinted away and then tried to pivot round quickly to come back. The edge of his cockpit dipped under the water, and the expression on his face – as the kayak filled with water and turned over – was so comical that Toby couldn't stop laughing.

'Kick yourself out!' called Julie. 'That's it. Keep hold of the kayak.'

She paddled over to Jay. 'Well done,' she told him. 'Now work your way to the front. Keep hold of the deck line. That's great. Now I've got your boat. You grab hold of my bow. How are you doing? OK?'

'Good,' said Jay, smiling. 'It's nice and cool in here.'

'Do you want to go to the side?' asked Julie. 'Or would you like to get back in here?'

'Can I?' asked Jay.

'I don't know,' she said. 'Let's find out.'

She brought the two boats together, side by side, with Jay's kayak facing backwards. Then she took a firm grip on the far side of Jay's boat and tilted her own kayak towards it. 'OK,' she said. 'Grab both boats and lie right back. That's it – look up at the sky. Now pop your feet up and into your cockpit. Now heave yourself up. Great! Well done!'

Jay thanked her and looked around, obviously very pleased with himself. 'Come on,' he said to Toby. 'I'll help you improve. I'm an expert now!'

Toby laughed. Jay had already helped him a lot with his swimming during their visits to the pool.

'Like this . . .' Jay went on. 'Follow behind me.'

Half an hour later, Rick and Julie brought all the Patrols together from the different parts of the lake where they had been working. Toby was starting to feel as if he was improving. He could go in a straight line – more or less – and Jay had shown him how to shift his weight as he made a turn. 'Not like I did when I fell in,' Jay explained.

'We're going to learn the sweep stroke now,' Rick told them. 'This will let you turn your boat in a controlled way.'

'Unlike Toby,' laughed Guy from the Panthers.

'Ignore him,' said Abby.

'Keep the blade of your paddle as far away from your body as you can . . .' Rick demonstrated, sweeping the paddle round in a wide circle from front to back so that his kayak spun neatly in the water. 'You can paddle backwards too,' he went on, 'and you turn in the opposite direction. You should all have a go, but remember to keep your weight centred. If you lean over too far, you know what'll happen!'

They practised sweep strokes for a while, and once again Toby found that he was beginning to feel more relaxed. 'It's good, isn't it?' he said to Connor when they drew alongside each other for a moment. 'You can feel the water though the bottom of the boat. It's a bit like skiing and skating and riding a bike. It's all about balance.'

'I guess,' Connor agreed. 'The others are all doing OK too. I have a feeling we'll make a good kayak team.'

'OK,' said Rick, calling the Scouts together in the middle of the lake, 'now you're going to find out just how solid and stable kayaks can be. Anyone fancy running around on top of the kayaks?'

'I don't think so,' said Toby. 'We'd fall in.'

'You'll be surprised,' Rick said. 'Get your kayaks together, side by side, in your Patrols. That's it. Now each of you grab hold of the cockpit of the kayak next to you. Lay your paddle across in front of you too. Great. Now you've got a raft. Let's have a game of tag. Two of you hop out of your kayaks.'

'Come on,' said Abby to Andy. 'Me and you. You be "it".'

The two friends heaved themselves out of their cockpits. 'Amazing!' said Abby. 'It's solid!'

'Yes, but I could still push you in!' laughed Andy, jumping from kayak to kayak in pursuit. The air filled with the sound of laughter, yells and an occasional splash as the Scouts took it in turns to pursue one another over their rafted kayaks.

'That's very cool,' said Toby breathlessly as Rick finally called a halt. 'I would never have believed it.'

'Rafted kayaks are incredibly stable,' Rick told them. 'Two of us once took an injured friend twenty-five kilometres down a river even bigger than the one you saw on the video by rafting our kayaks together. That's all the instruction for now. Take five minutes to practise whatever you like, then we'll need to start packing up.'

'OK,' said Toby. 'I'm going to practise going straight. I reckon that's the hardest thing of all . . .' And he paddled away.

He was concentrating so hard that he didn't hear the shouts away to his left. 'Hey, Toby . . . ! Get out of the way, you idiot!'

Abby was steaming towards him, her paddles flailing, with Andy in hot pursuit. She was looking back at Andy rather than where she was going. Toby tried to turn away, but Abby altered course at the same moment and the bow of her kayak crashed into his side.

All at once Toby was upside-down. Water filled his mouth and forced its way up his nose, but somehow he managed not to swallow. He could see nothing but churning water. Just for a second a feeling of panic overtook him. He was going to drown! He was under the water. He was stuck in this stupid boat.

But all the time another part of Toby's brain

was still working. He knew what to do. He'd read everything he could find about kayaking. He'd borrowed books from the library. He'd watched endless videos on YouTube. He knew he had to kick himself out of the cockpit, and he managed to do it.

He came up out of the water like a cork from a bottle, remembering just in time to grab hold of his kayak.

Rick and Julie were by his side in seconds. 'Are you OK, Toby?' asked Rick.

'Sure,' said Toby. 'It's like you said earlier – we're bound to fall out.'

'You didn't *fall* out,' Julie said sternly. 'Abby, Andy, come here.'

'I'm sorry,' Abby began. 'It was an accident. We couldn't . . .' Her voice tailed off when she saw the look on Rick's face. 'Sorry, Toby.'

'Falling out is one thing,' Rick told her. 'Being reckless and stupid is something else. A minute under the water and you could be dead. You understand, don't you? Andy? You were as much to blame as Abby, you know.'

'I know. Sorry, Toby. Sorry, everyone,' Andy said to the rest of the Tigers, who had gathered around in their kayaks.

'OK,' said Rick. 'That's over and done with then. One good thing came out of it. That was a textbook escape, Toby. You're out of the boat and you're safe. Well done. All you've got to do now is get back in.'

Even though he had watched Jay do it earlier, Toby still found the process of levering himself back into his kayak far harder than kicking himself out had been. By the time he was back in again, he discovered that all the others were already taking their boats out of the water. 'Can't I go for just one more paddle?' he asked Julie.

'Go on, then,' she said, laughing. 'You can come back to the shore the long way round. I would have thought you'd had enough of the water for one day!'

'I'm just starting to get the hang of it,' Toby said seriously. 'I don't want to forget how it feels.'

He paddled round in a wide circle. It was great to be the only kayak out on the lake. Now that he knew he could get out of his kayak safely, and get back in again, he felt far more confident. His boat wobbled alarmingly, and for a second he almost panicked, but it was OK. Without thinking, he took a shallow stroke with his left hand, and the kayak resumed its steady course. He coasted neatly to a stop beside the pontoon and found Jay waiting to help him out.

'I told you, didn't I?' said Jay as they lifted the kayak and carried it over to the trailer. 'Once you get the hang of it, it's like riding a bike. You won't ever forget.'

They stowed all the kayaks on the racks, and Rick, Julie and the helpers started strapping them in place. The Tigers sat together in the shade of a group of rowan trees. Bunches of berries hung down over their heads, already starting to turn orange and reminding them that summer was nearly over.

'I'm really sorry about the accident,' said Abby. 'I know I was stupid – I won't do it again. It's my August resolution. I'm going to be quiet and sensible for the rest of the time we're here.'

'You can't!' exclaimed Priya with a grin. 'That would be no fun at all.'

'Actually,' said Toby, 'I'm glad it happened. I was worrying about having an accident and capsizing, and now I know it's OK.'

'It's tough, getting back in on the water,' Jay said. 'We all ought to practise doing it if we get the chance.'

'I've got notes in one of my books,' said Toby. 'I'll show you if you like . . .' He started to open his rucksack.

'You haven't brought a notebook here, have you?' asked Connor in amazement.

'I like to write things down,' replied Toby. 'Like if I notice something important and I think I might forget. What's wrong with that?' he asked as he saw the others staring at him.

'Nothing,' replied Andy, shaking his head in disbelief. 'That must be why you know so much.'

CHAPTER 4

As soon as breakfast was over the following morning, Rick and Julie called the whole Troop together.

'Today we're going to do a survival exercise,' Rick told them. 'Lots of the things you do will count towards your Survival Skills Badge – but, more importantly, they might save your lives one day. You have fifteen minutes to sort out a day pack with anything you think might be useful for spending a night in the woods with no tent and no sleeping bag. And, Toby, just a normal-sized pack, please!'

There was laughter from the assembled Scouts, but Toby ignored it. He was too busy thinking about what to put in his rucksack. Rick hadn't said exactly what they would be doing, but it was a safe bet that they would be building some kind of shelter and lighting a fire. He was laying the essential items out on his sleeping bag when Jay poked his head into the tent they shared.

'This time you really *will* have to leave some things behind.' Jay laughed as he looked at the growing pile. 'I don't think you'll be allowed to take a stove – or the kitchen sink!'

Even without the pile of things on his sleeping bag, Toby's small rucksack was bulging fit to burst. 'There's one good thing . . .' he said to the others as they prepared to follow Rick and Julie along the forest path. 'At least I won't be going underwater today.'

'I certainly hope not,' said Julie, turning back to look at him and laughing. 'If you did fall in, that rucksack of yours would drag you right to the bottom.'

After walking for half an hour they reached a more open part of the forest. There were a few birch and rowan trees, along with some small oaks; bracken too, and brambles and nettles growing beneath the trees. They reached a clearing and the leaders paused.

'We've got a surprise for you,' said Rick. 'They should be here any minute now.'

As he spoke, Toby heard the sound of footsteps descending a steep track that led up to their right. Moments later, Chris Sutcliff appeared; beside him was a tall man dressed in khaki trousers and a safari jacket. There was a burst of excited chatter among the Scouts, for they all recognized this man. Clyde Churchill presented a popular survival show on TV. They were used to seeing him camping out in the middle of a desert or a jungle, but now he was here in real life!

'I used to do a bit of kayaking with Clyde when I was younger,' Rick said, smiling. 'He was in this part of the world so I persuaded him to come along and give us a little help today.'

Clyde put down the large cool box he'd been carrying. 'Nice to meet you guys. First thing I'm going to do is show you how to prepare fish for cooking on your fires. I hope that at least one of the members of your patrol has a sharp knife!'

He lifted a glistening silver fish out of the box and laid it down on the grass. 'If the fish is longer than about ten centimetres, you should gut it,' he said. 'But you'll need to bury the entrails, so have a hole ready dug.'

Clyde took a large knife from a sheath at his waist and made a hole in the grass, then used another knife to slit open the fish's stomach and clean out the guts. He put them in the hole, filled it neatly with soil and replaced the small piece of turf. 'There,' he said. 'Now I've left no trace. You can cook the fish how you like. You could wrap it in clay if you had some, and cook it in the embers. Or put it on a stick and cook it on top. The best way, if you have a pan, is to boil it – then you don't lose all the goodness just under the skin. There's plenty of fish here for you to cook later, but now I think you're going to make some shelters.'

'Thanks, Clyde,' said Rick before turning to the Scouts. 'We've prepared plenty of materials for you to use. If you were truly in the wild you'd have to find these yourselves, and possibly cut branches from living trees, but we'll only be using dead wood today – except for small green sticks, which you might need for cooking. You are allowed to cut bracken though, and you should be on the lookout for any wild food that's edible. We also have permission for you to remove turf to make a fire, but be sure you store it carefully so that you can leave this whole area exactly as you found it. Now, you must get your priorities right. You need to be able to keep warm and find food and water. You do everything as if you would really be spending the night in your shelters. Off you go.'

Most of the Patrols quickly moved off into the woods, chattering excitedly. Abby made to follow them, but Toby called her back. 'We ought to make sure we can find our way back,' he said. 'We know how easy it is to get lost in woods.'

'Sure,' said Abby, who had pulled a compass out of her pocket. 'That's why I brought this. South is that way— Hey, Andy, what are you doing?'

Andy had taken out his camcorder. 'I won't get many chances on this trip so I thought I'd make a movie about survival,' he said, pushing his long hair out of his eyes. 'I can't take this camera on the water. I really wish I had one of those waterproof ones Rick used in his movie.'

'You're crazy!' Abby gave him a friendly shove. 'Only you would have decided that a video camera was essential survival equipment. *Now* can we go?'

They made their way between their trees and soon found a small clearing where materials for shelter building had been stacked at regular intervals beneath the trees. 'Everyone has to do their own,' Connor said. 'Let's get started.'

Toby smiled to himself. He was almost sure that he would win this challenge. It might even make up for falling in the lake. He had already spotted two young trees that were just the right distance apart, and he quickly removed a square plastic sheet from his bag, threaded some cord through the holes at the corners and stretched the plastic low down between the trees. Then he folded the bottom half back to make a ground-sheet. He slipped inside to make sure it was a snug fit, then set off to collect some small branches and ferns. He propped branches against the ends of the shelter and tucked bracken in between them, then laid plenty more bracken on the floor and rolled inside. It was perfect.

He looked through the trees and saw Andy struggling to balance a long pole between two uprights. It collapsed three times before Andy finally made the structure secure and began laying short sticks and bracken over the top. Toby crawled out of his shelter and stood up.

Connor had nearly finished his own structure and was looking at Toby's. 'I might have known,' he said, laughing. 'It's nearly as good as a tent! That looks like the plastic sheet my parents use in the garden to collect hedge-trimmings.'

'It is!' replied Toby as the others joined them and admired his instant shelter. 'I . . . er . . . borrowed it from our shed. It's really light and hardly takes up any room in my bag.'

'Leaving you space for all the other stuff,' said Connor. 'I guess we'd better start the fireplace, then. No one else has finished yet.'

Toby selected a spot for the fire and took out

his penknife to dig out the turf. When he had removed a large square, he scraped away at the soil until he had made a shallow depression about ten centimetres deep. Connor had collected some small rocks from beneath the trees and made a neat edging around the hole. Then they started to search for firewood.

Before long the Tigers' shelters were complete. They had had plenty of practice at building these simple bivouacs during the year and had all done a good job.

'I'm going to build a circular fire,' Toby said. 'There's no point making a reflector fire. It would warm some of us but not the others. Can you help me make some tinder, Connor? Have you got your grandpa's knife?'

'You know I wouldn't go anywhere without it,' Connor replied, taking the old knife out of his pocket. 'I sharpened it specially.'

Connor and Toby set to work shaving fine strips from old, dry twigs. The other Tigers were busy making piles of firewood, graded neatly from small sticks to good-sized logs.

Toby glanced up at the sun, which was now high in the sky. 'You know what?' he said to the others. 'I reckon we can do it without matches.' He rummaged in his bag and pulled out a small magnifying glass. 'What do you think? It has to be worth a try.'

They all gathered round as Toby carefully placed a little ball of shavings in the middle of the fireplace, then held the magnifying glass so that a small, intense beam of light was concentrated on the tinder. It was only a few seconds before a slender column of smoke started rising into the air.

'Yes!' exclaimed Abby and Priya together.

Connor was on his hands and knees, blowing sideways at the shavings. Suddenly a tiny flame leaped up, and Jay began placing small twigs carefully on the fire. The Tigers were all so busy watching the flames grow that they didn't notice Rick and Julie enter their clearing until they were standing right behind them. Clyde was with them.

'I don't know if you learned this stuff from my

show, or from Rick and Julie here,' said Clyde, looking round at their shelters, 'but you've done a terrific job, guys! I especially like your use of plastic – I never travel without a tarpaulin like that!'

Toby felt himself reddening. 'I know,' he said. 'That was what gave me the idea.'

'Excellent! Now if you'll all come back to the clearing, I'd like to show you some of the things you can find to eat here in the woods.'

They followed Clyde, Rick and Julie back to where the rest of the Troop were looking carefully at the collection of edible plants and berries that Clyde had laid out for them.

'I collected all these things within a thousand metres of here,' he said. 'The river is about four hundred metres to the south, and that's where this wild garlic came from. It makes a perfect salad. There's sorrel too – take a look.'

They inspected all the leaves, sniffing the pungent odour of the wild garlic. 'There are quite a few blackberries as well,' Clyde told them. 'And even one or two raspberries – although you'll have to look hard to find them.'

'So . . . we don't have to eat worms?' asked Abby. 'Or lizards or snakes, like on your TV show?' She sounded almost disappointed.

Clyde laughed as one or two of the Scouts couldn't help shuddering. 'Believe me,' he said, 'if you're hungry enough, you'll eat just about anything. Some of the best things to eat are insects and grubs. They're packed full of protein. Worms are OK, but they're a bit earthy!'

'I'm hungry now,' said Jay. 'It must be lunch time.'

Rick and Julie exchanged amused glances.

'You're right,' Clyde said. 'I've brought you some special treats to try. I fried them up myself this morning.' He opened up another cool box as Connor's dad set up a folding table in front of him, and placed two large shallow dishes on the table.

'Grasshoppers and crickets,' Clyde announced with a grin. 'Oh, and I've made my special chilli dipping sauces.' He put three smaller bowls on the table. 'The one in the red cup is extremely hot,' he said. 'And I mean hot.'

'This time I'm not worried about the sauce,' said Toby. 'It's those I don't like the look of! He indicated the bowl of large brown insects. Legs were poking out everywhere, and heads, and eyes.

'Honestly,' said Priya. 'Don't make such a fuss! You eat prawns, don't you? These are just the same.'

She stepped forward, picked up a grasshopper, dipped it in the hottest chilli sauce and crunched it in two. Clyde raised his eyebrows and waited. Priya swallowed, then popped the rest of the insect in her mouth and swallowed again.

'Delicious!' she pronounced as other Scouts began stepping forward gingerly to try the grasshoppers. 'The chilli sauce is perfect!'

Clyde laughed. 'Rick, you have some very tough Scouts here! Come on, guys, there's plenty for everyone. And if you don't like the insects, I brought a few sandwiches too, just in case!'

'Make the most of your lunch,' said Rick. 'It's all you'll get today apart from what you cook for yourselves this evening – fish and baked potatoes and any other food you can find. But please remember, get your wild food checked by an expert before you eat it. Oh, and there's one more thing. You'll be sleeping right here in those shelters, so I hope they're as snug as they look!'

CHAPTER 5

In the morning Connor woke to the sound of birds chattering in the branches above his head. He felt stiff and uncomfortable as he rolled out of his shelter and stood up. The bracken on the floor had felt soft at first, but during the night the hard contours of the rocky ground had started pressing into his body. He looked around and stretched. It was already warm, even though it was still very early and the first rays of the sun were only just starting to catch the treetops.

He went over to the fireplace. The night before, they had carefully sealed the embers of the fire with a covering of earth, and now, when he carefully removed the crust, he found that they were still warm. He set to work with his penknife to make more shavings, and was just blowing the fire into life when he heard Priya's voice.

'That was just about the most uncomfortable night I've ever spent,' she muttered, rubbing her eyes. 'Oh good, the fire's still alive.'

Priya might have had a rough night, thought Connor, but for some reason her shorts and T-shirt weren't crumpled like his. The other Tigers crawled out of their shelters, groaning as they stretched and yawned.

'There's not much point in a fire,' said Abby. 'We haven't got anything to cook.'

'No,' said Toby, 'but I've got some tea bags, and we have plenty of water.'

It had been a good moment the previous afternoon when Connor had discovered that all the Tigers had put water purification tablets in their emergency packs. When Rick had come to their camp offering water to those who needed it, they had been able to show him their bottles, filled from the nearby stream and already purified.

'Nice one, Toby,' said Andy. 'But I don't see how we can boil water in plastic bottles.'

'We can use this . . .' said Toby. 'But only if you all promise never to laugh at my rucksack ever again.'

He brought out a battered old billycan and a cup. 'I didn't use them last night because we had to prove we could cook without pans,' he told them. 'But I don't see why we can't use them now.'

'Toby, you're a star!' said Abby. 'Let's get that water boiling.'

When Rick and Clyde came into the camp fifteen minutes later, the Tigers were discussing the meal they had cooked the evening before. Priya had proved to be easily the best at gutting and cleaning the fish, and Jay had designed an ingenious spit made from two Y-shaped sticks on either side of the fire with the fish skewered on another stick suspended between them, while the others had simply held their fish over the flames on sticks. 'I don't think it made any difference which way they were cooked,' Abby was saying. 'They all tasted delicious.'

'Well!' said Clyde. 'This isn't survival, this is

luxury! Looks very like the old billycan I take everywhere with me. Very neat!'

'The sleeping wasn't luxury,' said Abby. 'I hardly slept at all.'

'You've kept yourselves warm and dry,' said Clyde. 'If you ever find yourselves having to do it for real, that's what's going to matter.'

'And now you need to put this place back just the way you found it,' Rick said. 'We want it to look as if we had never been here. After that, you'll all be pleased to hear, you won't have to walk back to camp. We've brought the kayaks down here.'

It was mid-morning by the time the Scouts had carefully removed every trace of their presence. The other patrols set off one at a time; the Tigers were last into the water, with Julie to supervise them.

'This is great,' said Jay a few minutes later as they paddled upstream against the current. 'The water's moving faster than you think, isn't it?'

'Don't talk to me,' grunted Toby. 'I'm trying to keep in a straight line.'

'You're doing fine,' Jay told him with a laugh.

The nose of Toby's kayak wobbled to the right, and immediately he felt the river trying to force the boat round. He took a wide, shallow stroke and the bow came straight again.

'Good work, Toby!' called Julie from behind him. 'Keep it up. We'll carry on a little way round the bend. Keep your eyes peeled for tree branches and obstacles, and steer a course to avoid them. You go ahead, Connor.'

The Tigers paddled on for over an hour before they finally reached the campsite.

'That was terrific, all of you,' Julie said as they pulled the kayaks onto the bank. 'We'll take a short break for lunch, and then carry on up the river for a bit. Here . . .'

She tossed packets of sandwiches and bottles of drink to the Scouts and they all wolfed them down hungrily, eager to get back on the river.

'Ready?' said Julie when they had finished eating. 'Let's go.'

Half an hour later, she pointed her paddle towards a smooth patch of water to her left and they all assembled there. Toby discovered that his kayak was hardly moving.

'This is an eddy,' Julie told them. 'As the water flows downstream it hits rocks – and also the banks as it comes round the bends. If you look at the surface of the water you can see how different parts of the river are moving in different ways. Eddies like this are very useful to us because they give us a chance to take a break.'

'I can hear something,' said Priya. 'It sounds like—'

'It's rapids,' exclaimed Abby. 'Can we . . . ?'

'No,' said Julie with a smile. 'This is as far as we go today. The next stretch upstream is narrower and, as you've guessed, a bit rockier, although I wouldn't exactly call it rapids. We're just going to use this spot where the current is flowing a little faster to get the feel for what happens when you turn your kayak. I'll show you . . .'

Julie paddled a short distance downstream, then came back towards them and turned her kayak in a semicircle towards the opposite bank. 'Anyone notice anything?' she asked.

'You shifted your weight,' said Priya.

'Right,' agreed Julie. 'Whenever you're making a turn you need to keep your weight on the side nearest the centre of your turning circle. Tilt the boat the other way and you're sure to capsize. And if you do, remember you're using the spray-decks today. You'll have to kick that little bit harder to get out.'

The spraydecks were fastened around the rims of their cockpits, sealing the Tigers into their kayaks. Toby wondered nervously just how easy it was to detach them in an emergency. He watched carefully as the other Tigers copied Julie's manoeuvre. Connor and Priya made it look easy, but Andy forgot to paddle halfway through his turn and found himself slipping sideways downstream. Abby went at it full tilt, gave a dangerous-looking lurch in one direction, and somehow corrected it. Jay was next and had no trouble; then it was Toby's turn. He headed along, parallel to the bank, rehearsing what he was going to do in his head. *Don't forget to keep paddling*, he told himself. *Weight on the left side.*

He pulled on his left paddle and the bow began to turn. He was concentrating so hard that he didn't register the warning shouts from Julie and the other Tigers waiting in the eddy. He felt the river grab the bow of his kayak, and started paddling hard. The crash took him totally by surprise. It was like an explosion – a heavy thud on the side of his kayak and a loud cry of anger – and then he was on his side in the water, spinning round as another kayak flashed past him, paddles spinning furiously in the air.

'Kick, Toby!' yelled Julie.

And now, quite suddenly, Toby was upside-down in the green, turbulent gloom. He kicked, and then remembered the spraydeck. He tried to stay calm as he realized that he was going to need to kick harder. He was aware that he was still moving downstream, and spinning at the same time. He kicked again – and then he was free and he felt relief surge through him.

Suddenly there was a crunching impact, and something scraped painfully along Toby's side. He felt a bump against his helmet, and he twisted over to see the shape of his kayak, distorted by the green water, moving quickly past him. He tried to reach up and grab it, but something was very wrong. For some reason he couldn't move his foot.

He forced himself to think. Once again he turned under the water and reached out with his hand. Now he could see it: a tree had fallen into the river, and his foot was caught in one of its tangled branches. *I'm not hurt*, he told himself. *My foot got in there – I can get it out.*

How long had he been under the surface? Toby had no idea. It felt like for ever, but it could only have been a few seconds. As he grabbed hold of a stumpy projecting branch and pulled himself down, he wondered how long he could hold his breath. One minute? Two? He could feel his foot with his hand now. It was wedged tightly between two branches. He took hold of one of them and pulled, trying to release his foot from the trap. It was stuck fast. He yanked again and again, but it did no good, and now his lungs were bursting and something funny was happening to his eyes. This was so stupid. There had to be a way to get free . . .

Connor had watched Toby preparing to make his turn with a smile on his face.

'Look,' Abby said with a giggle. 'He's biting his lip.'

'He always does that when he's concentrating,' Jay pointed out as Toby began to turn. Suddenly, out of the corner of his eye, Connor was aware of a movement. A blue kayak flashed into view, travelling at top speed, paddle flailing like a windmill. Connor let out a yell of warning but it was too late. Toby was intent on his paddling and didn't even hear. The red-helmeted kayaker crashed into Toby's boat, tipping it onto its side. The kayaker called out angrily, glanced round and saw the small group waiting in the eddy, paddled a few metres further and then stopped, looking back.

Toby was on his side in the water. 'Kick!' Julie yelled.

'He knows what to do,' Connor said. 'He'll be OK.'

Then Toby's kayak turned over completely.

Julie, with Connor beside her, paddled swiftly after it. Connor saw movement. 'He's out!' he yelled. 'Well done, Toby!'

But as the kayak spun away downstream, there was no sign of the Tigers' Assistant Patrol Leader.

'Something's happened . . .' Connor's heart started pumping. He couldn't understand why Toby hadn't surfaced. He was aware of the others moving towards him, but Julie waved them back. He edged his kayak forward and saw something dark below the surface. 'It's a tree,' he called out. 'And I can see him. I can see Toby. His foot's caught. I'm going in.'

'Connor, wait!'

But Connor had already pulled off his buoyancy aid and manoeuvred his kayak downstream of the fallen tree. 'I'll be fine,' he said. 'It's clear below the tree. I can't get pushed against it by the current. Grab my kayak . . .'

He ignored Julie's protests and tumbled into

the river. He trod water for a moment, getting a feel for the current, then duck-dived and forced himself downwards. It was hard with the spray-deck ballooning around his waist. He saw a branch and took hold, slowly pulling himself further down towards Toby. He could see his friend clearly now, desperately attempting to free his foot – but as Toby pulled at his leg, he was tightening the tangle of branches and weed. Connor reached down and yanked Toby's foot towards him. Immediately the tangle became looser. He tugged at a branch and it came away in his hand. Another, and another – and suddenly Toby was free, rocketing up to the surface.

Connor followed him at once, and surfaced beside him, gasping air into his lungs.

'Hold onto my kayak, both of you,' Julie shouted.

Connor did as she said, and turned to see Toby coughing and retching. Seconds later they were back in the eddy and Julie was out of her kayak, pulling Toby onto the shore.

'I'm OK,' he gasped. 'I swallowed a bit of water, that's all.'

'You were under a long time,' Julie said, and Connor realized that her face was very pale under its tan.

The other Tigers were watching anxiously from their kayaks, and now the lone paddler in the red helmet approached them and said, 'There was nothing I could do . . . I couldn't avoid him.'

'Where are the rest of your party?' demanded Julie. 'You shouldn't be out on your own.'

The kayaker glanced upstream. 'They were just behind me – I . . .'

A blue kayak came round the bend in the river, followed by several more. Max, the Patrol Leader they'd met two nights before, was in the lead. When he saw his fellow Sea Scout, he gave a signal to those behind him and circled round. 'Sam?' he said. 'We're supposed to stay together. You know that. What happened?'

'Your friend came belting round that bend without paying attention,' said a grim-faced Julie. 'You might want to have a word with him.'

'Sam's a girl,' replied Max. 'I'm sure she didn't do it on purpose.'

'I didn't say she did,' replied Julie as the Sea Scouts' Leader joined the others, frowning beneath his helmet. He was a thin man with sharp brown eyes and a trace of stubble on his cheeks. As he manoeuvred his kayak, Connor saw powerful muscles ripple in his arms.

'Is everything, OK?' he asked.

'Not really,' said Julie. 'It would be a big help if you could keep your party together. I'm sure they'll tell you what happened.'

He looked at her for a moment. Connor had seen her angry before, when someone had done something stupid, but now she was really furious. 'Maybe it would be better if we discussed this later,' he said finally. 'I'll get this lot back, OK?'

The Sea Scouts moved off down the river. Sam hesitated for a moment. 'Look, I'm really sorry,' she said. 'I know I should have been looking. I'm a total idiot sometimes. And I thought that was awesome, what you did . . .' she told Connor, before spinning round and paddling rapidly after her friends.

'Hmm,' said Julie, watching her go. 'Maybe she's not such a bad girl after all.'

'No,' Abby retorted. 'She got it about right. She's an idiot.'

'She seems to like Connor, though,' said Priya with a sly grin, and Connor felt the colour rising to his cheeks.

He turned to Toby. 'Are you really sure you're OK,' he asked.

'Yeah,' said Toby, getting to his feet. 'I always knew I'd get out of it somehow. And I'm starving! Aren't the Kestrels cooking Chinese chicken?'

For the first time since the accident, Julie's face broke into a smile. 'Now I *know* you're OK,' she said, laughing. 'Come on, let's get you all back to the camp.'

CHAPTER 6

That evening, as the Tigers were on wood-chopping duty in the taped-off area close to their camp, they heard raised voices from the Sea Scouts' camp a short distance away along the riverbank.

'It's the Sea Scouts' Leader,' hissed Abby. 'Who's that he's talking to?'

'It's a canoe instructor,' Toby told them. 'He's called Phil and he's going to be leading our gorge walk tomorrow. Rick was talking to him earlier.'

'This part of the river seems to be getting a bit crowded,' the Scout Leader was saying. 'And that short stretch of white water isn't really enough for these guys. They've paddled far trickier stuff than this before now. If the river was higher it might be different, but . . .'

'Well, you'll have to make your own decision,

69

obviously,' Phil replied slowly, 'but if you go up beyond the waterfalls you'll need to take extra care.'

'Sure,' replied the Scout Leader. 'We know that. You're up for it, aren't you, guys . . . ?' It sounded as if he had turned away to talk to his Scouts, and his voice was soon out of earshot.

'Did you hear what he said about the river being crowded?' asked Toby as they moved away. 'That was us he was talking about.'

'I reckon it'll be better if they do go somewhere else,' Jay said. 'Unless you were hoping to see more of that girl, Connor?' he added with a smile as Connor came over to join them.

'What are you on about?' asked Connor.

Abby told him what they'd overheard. 'We'll have the river to ourselves if they go somewhere else. That's good, isn't it?'

'I don't know,' Connor answered thoughtfully. 'They seemed OK to me – I thought we might have made friends with them. It was an accident, after all, and accidents can happen to anyone.'

'Listen, Rick's got his guitar out,' interrupted

Toby, changing the subject. He was still feeling a bit shaky after what had happened earlier. He had been telling himself that he'd have got his foot free in time, but inside he wasn't *completely* sure. He'd never been so glad to see anyone as he was when he found Connor peering at him through the swirling water.

'Julie's got an enormous bag of marshmallows,' said Priya.

'And I'm still starving,' said Toby. 'It must be something to do with being underwater so often.'

Early the following afternoon the Matfield Scouts stood at the top of a waterfall, looking down into the seething foam twenty metres below. They had completed their gorge walk and were looking forward to their lunch. 'We just climbed that,' said Priya, her eyes full of excitement. 'Can you believe it?'

'It wasn't a *walk*, though, was it,' said Abby as they turned and headed upstream beside the rushing white water. 'It was climbing and swimming and generally getting wet!'

Shortly afterwards they reached a footbridge. The Tigers all paused to look at the white water upstream from them, and Connor could see that every one of them was wishing they could try kayaking on it.

'Sorry, guys,' said Rick, shaking his head as he joined them on the bridge. 'There isn't time to do everything. We have the hill walk tomorrow and then we're off down river in the kayaks.'

They sat beside the river munching on the ham, cheese and hummus-with-salad sandwiches that the Panthers had prepared that morning. 'I suppose the Panthers aren't all bad,' said Abby grudgingly, helping herself to an apple.

'Say that again for the camera,' Andy said. Connor's dad and Usha had driven two of the minibuses to the top of the gorge, ready to transport the Scouts back to camp. Dr Sutcliff had brought Andy's precious camcorder with him so that Andy could shoot some footage of the waterfalls. He pointed the lens at Abby's face and she stuck her tongue out.

Suddenly Connor saw Abby's face change.

'Look!' she gasped. 'Where are they going?'

Connor spun round, just in time to see a blue boat flashing under the wooden footbridge. The red-helmeted kayaker was paddling furiously as the current caught the kayak and spun it round, carrying it backwards down the fastest part of the river, directly towards the top of the waterfall.

'Paddle!' Connor found himself on his feet and shouting, but Abby had reacted even faster than Rick and Julie.

'Abby, be careful!' they shouted after her as she leaped from rock to rock, out towards the middle of the river where the water was funnelled into a narrow channel before it soared over the edge of the cliff.

The kayaker was still frantically trying to escape from the onrushing current. Just for a moment Connor thought he'd been successful as he fought his way towards the far bank, but suddenly the bow of the kayak collided with a rock and it spun round and almost capsized. Somehow the kayaker stayed upright, and was now, for the first time, directly facing towards the

Scouts on the bank. Suddenly Connor realized that it was Sam, the girl who had crashed into Toby the day before. As she was swept along towards the top of the waterfall, she never once stopped paddling, fighting against the current all the way. Then she saw Abby . . .

Abby had flung herself full-length across the rocks so that she could reach out over the surface of the water. Rick and Julie were right behind her and, with a quick glance at each other, they knelt down and took hold of her feet.

Connor started towards her, but his dad was beside him and held him back. 'They're on it,' he said. 'We'd only get in the way.'

Sam was paddling desperately now. She was ten metres away . . . five metres. The current threatened to carry her away beyond Abby's outstretched arms, but at the last moment she spun the kayak round, and just for a second the stern came within reach. Abby seized hold and tugged the boat towards her. Connor saw that her knuckles were white as she struggled to hang on, but suddenly Rick reached past her and hooked his fingers over the cockpit. Moments later he had Sam in his arms, and Julie and Abby were pulling the kayak out of the water.

It was the evening of the same day, and the twilight had brought some welcome relief from the sultry heat. The Tigers were sitting with their feet dangling in the river when they saw a group of Sea Scouts approaching.

'We want to thank you for what you did,' said Max.

'And to say sorry for the other day,' Sam put in. She wasn't much taller than Priya, Toby realized, and she had a sparky look about her that reminded him very much of Abby. 'I keep messing up,' Sam continued. 'It was so stupid, what happened today. I just didn't listen when Joey, our Scout Leader, told us where to stop, and then I didn't hear him calling me back – and then it was too late. I mean, I don't want you to think that we go around doing completely crazy things on purpose . . .'

'No,' agreed Max. 'Because we wanted to ask if

you'd like to come out kayaking with us tomorrow. We'll be on a much safer stretch of water, but it's still fast. Grade Three. What do you think?'

Toby saw Abby turn to Connor, her eyes shining. 'What are you waiting for?' she demanded. '*Of course* we have to go.'

'We'll have to ask Rick,' Connor began.

'Our Scout Leader has done it already,' Max told them. 'We've booked extra instructors, and he's happy for you to come. If you want to, that is?'

'Come on, Connor,' urged Abby. 'Say yes. We all want to go.' She looked around at the others, her eyes daring them to disagree.

Priya wasn't going to say no – and nor were Jay and Andy. Toby looked at them all and shrugged.

'OK, then,' Connor said finally, to a cheer from the Tigers. 'We all want to try kayaking on white water. We thought we wouldn't get the chance.'

Half an hour later the Tigers were still deep in

conversation with their new friends, eager for every bit of the Sea Scouts' kayaking experience.

'We've told you everything about *us*,' Sam said suddenly. 'Joey said they call you the Survival Squad. What's that about?'

'It's just a joke,' Toby said, embarrassed. 'Things keep happening to us. It's not our fault.'

Reluctantly the Tigers described the adventures they'd had during the past year. The Sea Scouts' mouths fell open as Andy described the climax of their cycling adventure, when they'd tackled a band of sheep-rustlers in the middle of the night in a remote Welsh valley.

'I don't believe it,' said Sam. 'You are *so* lucky.'

'We didn't *feel* lucky,' Priya told her. 'It was scary.'

'Yes, but even so—'

'Listen,' said Connor. 'What's that?'

Somewhere in the distance they heard a low roll of thunder and Toby wondered if it meant rain. 'We're going to tell ghost stories around the fire,' he told the Sea Scouts, glad of a chance to change the subject. 'You haven't been properly scared until you've heard Julie's stories.'

The following morning Rick and the Tigers loaded their kayaks onto the trailer behind one of the minibuses. The other Scouts gave them cheerful but envious waves as they stowed their loaded rucksacks in the other minibuses and headed for the mountains for a hill walk with Julie, Chris and the other adult helpers.

'I know what I'd rather be doing,' Jay said as he watched them go. 'It's going to be so hot!'

'Maybe not,' said Toby. 'It still looks cloudy over the hills. There must have been some rain up there. The river was definitely higher this morning.'

'You're right,' said Joey. 'They had four millimetres. I just picked up the weather report. All that thunder didn't come to much, but the downpour has made quite a difference to the river. Let's go . . .'

When they arrived, Toby looked at the river and couldn't help feeling disappointed. 'I thought it was meant to be white water,' Abby said as she stood beside him on the bank. The river was narrower here than it had been further down the valley, but it slid smoothly past them without a trace of white foam or rocks.

'You'll see,' Max said with a laugh. 'We came here last year. That water is faster than it looks and you'll get a surprise once we're round the bend. That's if you don't fall in before you get there!'

'I won't!' Abby began indignantly.

Toby laughed as Max went off to collect his kayak. 'You never learn, do you?' he said as Abby flicked her brown hair back and pulled on her helmet. 'Anyone could wind you up.'

She stuck her tongue out at him. 'It won't be me who falls in,' she said. 'It'll almost certainly be you.'

Connor started checking Toby's gear and Rick looked on approvingly. Out of the corner of his eye Toby saw that all the other Tigers were checking each other's equipment – working as a team. Toby did up his helmet and settled into his kayak as Connor held it against the bank. He gave a nod, and Connor let go. Instantly he found himself fighting to keep the boat on course.

'Stay by the right bank,' Rick called as Toby paddled determinedly into the current. He soon found the quieter water, and as he came out of the bend he saw the Sea Scouts gathered in a broad eddy. Beyond them, the river roared in a jumble of white foam.

Toby joined the Sea Scouts and waited for the other Tigers to arrive. Abby and Rick appeared some time after the others. Abby's hair was dripping under her helmet. 'I didn't go right in,' she said in explanation. 'Just onto my side – and I managed to get up again.'

'OK, then,' said Joey. 'The first thing we're going to show you is how to make a ferry turn across the river. Sam can demonstrate – she's an expert.'

Sam set off upstream, paddling hard against the increasing current. At a certain point she headed directly into the middle of the fastest water.

'See where she's looking,' said Max. 'Directly at the opposite bank, where she wants to go.'

Toby saw the current seize the bow of Sam's kayak and push it back downstream on the other side of the river.

'She makes it look easy,' Joey warned them, 'but don't be fooled. You saw how the current took the boat as soon as the nose started to turn. You need to be ready to show the bottom of your kayak to the current. If you tilt the wrong way, you'll go under. Who'd like to try next?'

'How about it, Toby?' asked Connor. 'Want to go first again?'

'OK,' he replied. 'Why not?'

He knew exactly what he had to do, but still the force of the river caught him by surprise as he hit the fastest part of the flow. Before he knew it, his boat had spun completely on its axis and he was careering downstream. He paddled furiously, and somehow found himself up against the bank in calmer water.

Joey paddled over to him. 'Well done!' he said.

Toby shook his head. 'I messed it up. I forgot to look where I was going.'

'Right.' The Scout Leader nodded approvingly. 'You know what you did wrong. That's great. Even better, you never once stopped paddling. Good work!'

Toby felt absurdly pleased. He paddled upstream to join Sam and watched as the Tigers crossed the river one by one. After practising for half an hour they took a break to eat their lunch, perched on rocks among the heather that was just coming into bloom, filling the air with a scent of honey.

'Are you ready to try the rapids, then?' asked Sam, and the Tigers all nodded eagerly.

'We don't have to paddle up there, do we?' asked Priya, looking at the white water.

'You can try if you like,' Sam told her.

'OK,' said Priya, 'but it looks difficult.'

'Stop teasing her, Sam,' interrupted Max, flashing Priya a smile. 'We carry the kayaks to the head of the rapids. Mind you,' he added to Sam, 'if anyone could do it, I bet Priya could. She's a complete natural.'

Priya blushed under her dark skin and the other Tigers laughed. They carried their kayaks along a narrow path through the heather to a place where, as Toby could see from the marks on the ground, other people had launched their boats before them.

'Come up here,' called Joey from a rocky outcrop above them. 'You can get a good look at the route you need to take. Try to keep to the right as much as possible. Chances are you'll get flipped round and find yourselves going backwards. Just remember . . .'

'Keep paddling!' chorused the Tigers.

They watched from their vantage point as the Sea Scouts barrelled through the rapids, making it look very easy indeed.

'Are you going first again?' Connor asked Toby.

'I think I'll let someone else do it this time,' Toby said, feeling self-conscious.

'Well, I'm going last,' said Andy, brushing his floppy hair out of his eyes. 'This is a perfect place to film from, so I'm going to shoot all of you and then I'll go.'

'I'll do it,' said Priya. 'I can't wait.'

'Good,' approved Connor. 'Max was right. 'You're definitely the best at this. Are you ready?'

Priya slipped into her boat, paddled out into the current and was instantly whipped away downstream. Toby clenched his fists by his side as spray broke over her head and she was suddenly travelling backwards, paddling furiously all the while. She bounced off the bank and turned the right way round again, still paddling as she burst out of the rapids into the calmer water beyond, where the Sea Scouts were waiting and cheering.

Priya punched the air and Abby launched herself from the bank, arriving seconds later, breathless and elated at the end of her run. Toby followed her, tense with excitement. He felt the water seize his kayak, and paddled for all he was worth. He didn't have time to think. All he could do was paddle. One moment he was going backwards; then he saw a rock looming in front of him and remembered Joey saying to hug the rocks, so he stayed close, ran over some bumpy water – and then he was through, and yelling with excitement and punching the air just as Priya had done.

Connor and Jay joined them, and then there was a long wait for Andy to put his camcorder away safely and make his own run.

'Want to do it again?' asked Max, grinning hugely.

'You bet!' exclaimed Priya, and the others laughed. 'I never want to stop!'

CHAPTER 7

Connor awoke in the night to the sound of rain pattering on the tent, but the air was still humid and sticky and he lay, half in and half out of his sleeping bag, thinking about the previous day and worrying about the expedition. If there was a lot of rain, the river might rise. They might not even be able to set out . . .

The Tigers and the Sea Scouts had arrived back at camp exhausted after spending the whole afternoon shooting the rapids and carrying their kayaks back to the top. When Connor had finished his last run, he'd stood with Max, the Sea Scouts' Patrol Leader, and Joey and Rick, and watched the other Tigers make their runs.

'You know what?' Max had said as Priya skilfully picked a perfect line through the tumbling water. 'That girl is just amazing. She looks like she's been doing it all her life. And the rest of your team aren't bad either.'

Rick and Joey had agreed with him, and Connor had felt truly proud of the Tigers. But this rain – a louder flurry of raindrops spattered the tent – if only it would stop . . .

Last night around the campfire Rick had told the Troop that he would be setting off very early in the morning with one of the patrols in order to set up some activities on the bivouac site down-river. Then he had drawn lots to decide which patrol would accompany him. The Tigers had cheered when they'd won, and there had been one or two muttered complaints from the other patrols, but then Rick had smiled and told them to be ready to leave at 05.30 hours.

'You're not serious?' Abby had exclaimed, groaning when Rick's face told her that he was.

There had been plenty of laughter from the other patrols, some of whom were already starting to fall asleep after their trip into the hills. 'We'll be thinking of you when we're having our break-fast at eight o'clock,' laughed Sajiv.

'I'll be thinking of you at *seven* o'clock when I'm still lying in my sleeping bag,' Kerry said, yawning. 'I'm ready for bed right now.'

Connor pressed the button on his watch that made it light up. Three o'clock. Another two hours. He had to try and sleep. At least the rain seemed to have stopped. There hadn't been much . . .

He woke with a start and realized that daylight was seeping though the tent. It was nearly five o'clock. He switched off his alarm before it could go off, and reached over to shake Andy awake.

'What is it? What's going on?' Andy mumbled sleepily.

'Time to get up,' Connor said. 'Come on – we have to get the fire going and make porridge.'

Andy groaned again, but started to pull himself out of his sleeping bag. Connor unzipped the tent and crawled out into a very different kind of morning. The air was filled with a damp, drizzly mist, and it actually felt cool. The trees were dripping gently onto the grass. Quickly

Connor washed and lit a fire in one of the cooking altars.

'What do you think?' Andy asked, pouring water into a smoke-blackened saucepan. 'Will we be able to go?'

'I guess it'll depend on the forecast,' Connor replied, mixing in a few handfuls of oats and a pinch of salt. 'I haven't seen Rick yet, have you?' He stirred the porridge, and soon it was bubbling away nicely.

Andy shook his head as the other Tigers joined them. They each had a dry bag with a few essential items in it – sleeping bag, spare warm clothing and plastic tarps which Rick had handed them with a smile the previous evening.

'We'll be bivouacking,' he'd said. 'So I thought we'd take a leaf out of Toby's book and use these! Have you all put sleeping mats in? Good. This will seem like luxury after your bivvy in the woods.'

Mysteriously, Toby seemed to have packed twice as much as the others. 'Your kayak will sink,' Abby told him. 'You know we're supposed to be travelling light.'

Toby grinned ruefully. 'I know,' he said. 'But honestly, everything I've got in there is completely essential.'

The others laughed. Connor knew that there was a difficult balance to be struck between being ready for anything and weighing yourself down with too much stuff, but he had to admit that Toby often had the very thing they needed in an emergency. He felt his own pocket to check that he had his Swiss Army knife. That really *was* an essential item.

The porridge was cooked, and Andy doled it out into the waiting bowls, which the Tigers grabbed eagerly.

Connor looked at his watch. 'Where's Rick?' he wondered. 'He's never late and it's almost time to leave.'

They all shook their heads, mouths too full to answer.

Then Connor saw the Scout Leader walking across the clearing with his phone clasped to his ear. As he approached, he switched it off, shaking his head. 'I can't get through to the weather station,' he told them. 'I've been trying for half an hour.' Andy handed him a steaming bowl of porridge and he sat down on a log. 'Mmmm, that smells good. Thanks, Andy.'

'So, are we going?' asked Connor.

Rick nodded and swallowed a mouthful. 'I've checked the update on the notice board at the Kayak Centre. The river's a little higher than it was, but not by a lot. There was some rain in the night, but I don't think it amounted to much. We'll make a start, and I'll try to get through to the weather people again shortly. We should reach our campsite by eleven, and the others will arrive in time for lunch.'

Toby had been sitting quietly, eating his breakfast. He had been thinking. The weather had definitely changed and a breeze had sprung up, just stirring the leaves of the trees. He found himself wondering if Rick was right to set off, and he nearly said something – but then he told himself he was being foolish. Rick had years of experience, and if he said it was safe, then obviously it was.

Toby stowed his bulky dry bag in the bow of his kayak. He had already sneaked an extra one in. He was pretty sure he'd thought of everything, but then his eyes fell on some rope lying with the canes they'd used to build their camp gateway. It wasn't heavy – there would be no harm in taking it. It might come in useful when they were building a shelter. He stowed the rope quickly, wedging it in beside his bag.

They were all ready now, their helmets on, paddles at the ready. Rick pulled out his phone and made one last attempt to get a weather update before shrugging his shoulders and stowing it away in his dry bag.

'Right then,' he said. 'I'll lead the way, and Connor – you bring up the rear. Remember, keep together and look out for each other. No fancy stuff. No rushing . . .' This last with a glance at Abby.

She shook her head. 'Don't worry,' she said.

'After what nearly happened to Sam I'm going to take it easy.'

One at a time they slid into their kayaks, fastened their spraydecks and waited in the wide, flat eddy by the bank. They were about to leave when Toby heard a shout and looked up to see the Sea Scouts running across the grass towards them.

'Good luck!' called Sam. 'Have a great trip!'

'See you!' called Max. 'Keep in touch. Come and visit us some time and we can go sea-kayaking.'

The Tigers all shouted their goodbyes. Somehow, Toby thought as Rick steered his kayak out into the main current, saying goodbye made it seem more like a proper voyage.

Abby followed Rick, then Abby and Jay, and now it was his turn. Two quick strokes and he was out in the river. At once he sensed that it had changed. It felt more powerful; very different from the relatively gentle stretch of water they had paddled on a couple of days earlier. It was moving fast – it was surprising how a couple of extra centimetres made it feel so much bigger. Toby began to make calculations in his head as he followed the string of kayaks downstream. The river was maybe ten metres wide. How much extra water would there be if it was an extra centimetre deep. Each square metre would—

'Toby!' Connor yelled from behind him. 'Watch where you're going! You'll hit the bank!'

Toby saw where he was heading and made a quick correction without even thinking. This water was moving fast – even faster now than it had been just five minutes before when they'd started. He was going to have to concentrate. He still didn't know exactly how much more water there was, but it was a lot.

Ten minutes later they reached the spot where they had bivouacked for the night. They passed it in a flash, and before long, rocky cliffs appeared on either side of them. They all followed Rick as he steered a course through the slower parts of the river, but even there the water was flowing quickly. However, all the Tigers were paddling confidently and Toby could tell that they were covering the distance very fast. Another fifteen minutes went by. 'We'll get there early,' he shouted to Connor, who was close behind him.

'Cool,' said Connor. 'Then we can have an easy day!'

'I don't know about that,' replied Toby. 'I don't think Rick will let us just sit around. Hey, look – he's stopping.'

Ahead of them, Rick had paused in an eddy close in under the left bank. The Tigers all joined him there, and Toby saw him watching them all carefully. 'Good work, Tigers,' he said. 'It looks as if all that practice you did yesterday has paid off. But I still don't understand why the river is rising like this. I'm going to try and call in again now.'

The Tigers exchanged anxious looks as Rick extracted the phone from his bag and hit the buttons. Toby watched the water lapping at a rock beside the bank. He was almost sure he could actually see it rising, but maybe it was just the wind making waves.

'At last,' Rick said into the phone. 'I've been trying to get you for nearly an hour. I checked the update on the noticeboard but the river's definitely rising . . . What? Yesterday's? So what's the latest on the river?' There was a long pause as Rick listened. 'But we've already set out,' he said. 'I guess we're about six kilometres downstream from the campsite at Ravensgill . . . Yes, I know that. Thanks.'

He switched off the phone and turned to the Scouts. He was looking very thoughtful. 'It's bad news, I'm afraid. The update I read was yesterday's. Phil was delayed posting today's, but I can't believe I didn't check the date. There's been heavy rain in the mountains and they say we have to get off the river as soon as we can. There's just one small problem.'

'What?' asked Connor. 'What problem?'

'There *isn't* anywhere to get out,' Toby said. 'Not between here and the place where we're going to camp. These cliffs go on for several kilometres.'

'But we can just go back,' said Priya. 'Can't we?'

'This current is very fast,' Rick told her. 'And

it's going to get faster. I know we haven't been travelling for long, but I think it would take too long to go back, even to where we camped the other day. That current is probably travelling at about seven kph and I doubt if you can paddle much faster than that flat out. I think the best option is to carry on. We should reach the place where we're going to camp in a couple of hours.'

Toby glanced down at the rock he'd been watching a couple of minutes earlier. It had vanished. A pang of anxiety twisted at his gut. 'The river is rising very fast,' he said to Rick. 'At least five centimetres just while we've been sitting here.'

'All right,' Rick admitted, 'I made a mistake back there. I wish I hadn't, but even leaders make them sometimes. There's no point worrying about it – we just have to deal with the situation. The sooner we do this, the better. Same order as before, and make sure you all concentrate all the time. With luck we'll soon be off the water.'

'We don't have a choice, do we?' Connor said, studying the worried faces of the other Tigers. 'As long as we look out for each other, we'll be OK. We've got Rick with us, and we all know he's paddled on much bigger rivers than this. We are the Survival Squad, after all.'

They all smiled nervously.

Rick looked seriously at them all in turn. 'Go exactly where I go,' he told them. And with that he paddled off, quickly followed by the Tigers. The current seized their kayaks and swept them along downstream.

CHAPTER 8

Connor watched the Tigers as they paddled along in front of him. He knew they were all scared by the situation, but not one of them had hesitated before heading out onto the rising water. This stretch didn't seem so bad; but then, as he glanced across at the far bank, he realized just how fast the trees were sliding past him. There was a shout from in front and he saw Rick pointing to an area of flat water. They all joined him there.

'I'd like you to take the lead now, Connor,' he said. 'That way I'm in a better position to help if I see anything go wrong. Not that it will, of course. Ready? Let's move.'

Connor set off. His heart was beating fast, but he didn't question the good sense of Rick's change of plan. And if Rick was not going to lead, then someone else had to do it. All the same, it was scary; his kayak was moving fast and he had to pick the route. The river curved round to the right and the cliffs rose higher on the left-hand side. He steered for the opposite bank, where the water was flowing a little more slowly. He felt opposing currents tugging at the kayak as the turbulent water twisted and turned, deflected by jumbled rocks beneath the surface. There was one! He steered close beside it, glancing down to see it flash past.

They were almost round the bend now and a new stretch of river began to open up. Connor glanced ahead, trying to find a path through the swirling water. He drew closer to the bank, and there was a sudden jolt. His kayak spun round and tilted alarmingly, snagged on something below the surface. He paddled madly – and suddenly the kayak was free again, spinning away backwards down the river. There was another jolt and he knew that he'd hit a rock. There was nothing he could do to stop himself as the kayak tipped onto its side and his head went under the surface.

He was upside down and he had no idea which way he was facing or what was happening. He forced himself to think as he saw a rock flash past uncomfortably close beside him. He could kick himself out of the kayak, but then the kayak would probably be lost with the river flowing so fast. Or he could try and right himself. Sam and Max had given them a demonstration of how to do it the day before, but there had been no time for the Tigers to have a go. He tried to remember what Joey had said as they'd watched the two Sea Scouts roll their kayaks in a quiet eddy below the rapids:

If you capsize, just take a moment to orientate yourself. Keep calm. Now watch . . . Paddles out of the water. Paddle to the rear. Then – you can't see it, but Max has put his head down to the spraydeck and he snaps the boat upright with his hips.

It took less than a second for all this to pass through Connor's mind. He knew the theory, but could he actually do it? He had to try. He was definitely upside down, and drifting fast. He pushed the whole paddle up out of the water along the side of the boat, trying to visualize what Max and Sam had done. It was almost impossible. He'd just have to try. He dug in his paddle, bent forward and snapped up from the hips – all at the same time. And suddenly he was upright, water streaming off his helmet.

'Connor!' yelled Rick, paddling full-tilt towards him. 'Are you OK?'

Connor couldn't speak, much less yell. He was too busy gulping air into his lungs. He took a hand briefly off his paddle and gave a thumbs-up.

Rick came up beside him for a moment, holding their boats together. 'You didn't swallow any water?'

'Honestly, Rick, I'm fine.'

'Well, that was a pretty neat roll. Where did you learn to do that?'

'We saw Sam and Max doing them yesterday, remember?'

'You mean you've never done one before?'

'No – but I thought I might as well have a go. Better than losing the boat.'

Rick grinned suddenly. 'Nice one, Connor. What tipped you over?'

'A tree under the water, I think. We need to watch out for them.'

'OK,' Rick said, breaking away and paddling upstream to let the other Tigers pass him. 'Carry on, Connor. Good job, mate!'

Connor glanced back to see the rest of the red-helmeted Tigers coming round the bend in the river. Priya was closest, her dark face a mask of concentration as she adjusted her course.

This is a big river now, he thought. *And it's getting bigger all the time.*

'That was close!' came Priya's voice from behind him. 'Nice escape!'

'I was lucky,' Connor called back over the roar of the river. 'If we hadn't watched the others yesterday I wouldn't have had a clue what to do.'

He was glad to hear the sound of Priya's voice. The river really *was* getting louder now. He tried to recall the map he'd looked at the night before in Toby's tent. Surely they would be out of this gorge section soon? The noise was now echoing off the rocky walls on either side. And then he saw where the new sound was coming from, and felt panic welling up inside him.

Up ahead, the banks drew closer together, forcing the water through a narrow passage between the cliffs. In a flash Connor remembered talking to the Sea Scouts the day before, as they'd stood looking down at the rapids. 'There's only one stretch of white water on your whole journey,' Max had said with a laugh, 'and it's nothing like this. You'll probably go straight through it without even noticing.'

Well, thought Connor grimly, *Max got that one wrong*. They would have to stop and rethink. He needed to find an eddy before they were swept into the onrushing torrent between the overhanging cliffs . . . There! A hundred metres away, under the left bank, he could see a place. There was another to his right, but the one on the left was closer. He headed directly for it, but only just made it. They were travelling terrifyingly fast, and he had an anxious wait as the other Tigers, and finally Rick, followed him into the quieter water.

'Well done, Connor,' Rick said. 'Excellent decision. And now we have a hard choice to make. You sure you're OK after that roll?'

'That was really cool,' said Jay. 'I want to try it.'

'Me too,' chorused the other Tigers.

'Don't even think about it,' warned Rick. 'This is not the place to start fooling around.'

'This is the last difficult bit, isn't it?' asked Toby after a brief silence. 'Once we're through here the land is much flatter. We'll be safe.'

'Maybe,' said Rick, eyeing the turbulent water ahead of them.

'I've got a map,' said Toby suddenly. 'I'll show you.'

'A map!' they all exclaimed together.

'It'll be all soggy.' Abby took off her helmet and tied her unruly hair back more firmly.

By way of an answer Toby felt under his buoyancy aid into a pocket in his jacket and pulled out a postcard-sized section of map, neatly laminated.

Connor shook his head. 'I might have known,'

he said. 'How did you know which bit of map to laminate?'

'I did them all before we left,' Toby replied. 'I cut out all the places I thought we were most likely to go. It's much better than carrying a whole map around, you know.'

'Show me . . .' said Rick. 'As you're so well-prepared, Toby, I guess I'd better take a look.'

'I know it's fast,' put in Priya as Rick inspected the map, 'but it's no faster than the stretch we were kayaking on yesterday, is it?'

'No,' replied Rick, looking up. 'But there's an awful lot more water funnelling through there. It'll feel very different. I know you could do it, but I reckon we should think about getting off the river and waiting this out. It hasn't finished rising yet, you know. Although Toby's right, of course. This is the only difficult section. The river cuts through a band of rock here, and then flows out onto the plain.'

'So what shall we do?' asked Jay. He, Andy and Abby had been very quiet, Connor noticed. 'We can't get off the river here.'

They all looked up at the sheer rock face behind them.

'We should explore the other side,' Rick said. 'It looks as if the cliffs are a fair way back from the river over there. We may be able to find a safe place to wait.'

Connor felt bad. He'd made the wrong decision after all. 'I'm sorry, Rick,' he said. 'I should have headed for that side.'

'You weren't to know,' Rick told him. 'And it's not a problem. You all did dozens of ferries yesterday, and as Priya says, this water's no faster. I'll go across and check that landing place out. If it looks OK, I'll come back and supervise you all across. Meanwhile you wait here and watch where I go. I'm going to head fifty metres upstream before I cross. I don't want to be too close to that lot.' He nodded towards the torrent surging between the cliffs, and set off upstream, keeping to the slower water close to the bank as much as he could.

'I'm going to get a shot of this,' said Andy.

The others turned to him in surprise. 'You've

never brought your camcorder!' said Abby, putting her helmet back on.

'As if!' replied Andy. 'No, I bought some disposable cameras from the motorway services when we stopped on the way here.' He pulled a small green camera out of a pocket and took a careful snap of Rick making his way with some difficulty against the current. 'Hey, get a bit closer together, you lot. I'll take one of you.'

The Tigers pulled their boats together. Connor was in the middle, with Abby and Priya on one side and Toby and Jay on the other. He peered past Andy, trying to see how far Rick had got. 'Hurry up, Andy,' he said. 'And don't fall in, you idiot,' he added as Andy took both hands off his paddle to take the picture and wobbled dangerously.

'Smile, then,' said Andy, and Connor laughed in spite of himself as the camera shutter clicked. It was great that the Tigers always managed to stay cheerful, even in difficult situations, he thought.

'Rick's going across,' said Priya. 'Wow! Look

how hard he's paddling!'

Connor could see that as soon as Rick had moved out into the main part of the river he was having to paddle flat out just to maintain his position. Rick looked over at the spot where he was heading, but then the current started to turn his kayak, and within seconds he was across the fastest-flowing section and shooting towards the opposite bank. Keeping close to the side, he headed back downstream towards the eddy, directly opposite where the Tigers were waiting. He was still travelling fast beneath the over-hanging trees when he gave a sudden cry: his kayak tipped onto its side and he clutched frantically at his jacket.

'What is it?' cried Priya in alarm. 'What's happened?'

'I don't know,' Connor began; then he stopped as he saw Rick's spraydeck coming away from his kayak.

Abby screamed as Rick kicked out frantically, trying to hang onto the kayak with his feet, but in vain. He was in the water now, still grabbing at his shoulder, mouth open as he rolled in the water. Then the current slammed him against the bank.

His kayak spun away downstream in the swirling water.

CHAPTER 9

'I'm going over,' said Connor. 'Priya and Andy, you come with me.'

'What about us?' asked Jay.

'You stay here. Andy and Priya are the strongest paddlers and there's no time to waste,' said Connor. 'Rick's heavy. I won't be able to help him on my own. Come on, you two, let's move.'

He led the way upstream, his heart pounding with anxiety. He could hear the others calling, their yells rising above the ever-present noise of the rapids. He could see now why it had taken Rick so long to make his way upstream. He had to paddle very hard to make any progress at all. He glanced across at the other side, picking a spot to aim for. He still couldn't understand what had happened to Rick – he couldn't see any obvious dangers.

'Can you see that big rock shaped like a triangle?' he called back to Priya and Andy, glancing quickly over his shoulder at their worried faces and indicating the rock with his head. They both nodded. 'That's what we aim for. Then we'll make our way along the bank as carefully as we can, OK? And watch out. Something tipped Rick out of his kayak and we still don't know what it was.'

Connor didn't waste any more time, but pointed his kayak into the onrushing water and paddled flat out towards the centre of the river, where the current was fastest. The kayak turned quickly, and Connor fixed his eyes on the triangular rock as his paddles spun through the water, showing the bottom of his kayak to the current. Just for a moment a jolt of exhilaration went through him as he headed swiftly towards the rock, but then he felt guilty. This was no time to be enjoying himself.

As he entered the slower water close to the bank, he turned to see Priya coming across. She made the turn neatly and without fuss, just as he'd known she would. Andy followed behind her. His kayak started to turn and Connor saw his eyes flick downstream, towards the place where Rick had fallen in. Instantly, the boat was turning too quickly.

'Andy!' Connor yelled. 'Paddle!'

Andy's eyes swung back to Connor and Priya, and somehow he managed to re-direct his kayak – though for one brief moment Connor's heart was in his mouth as a patch of rough water threatened to spin Andy off course again.

'Sorry,' Andy said, breathing hard as he caught up with the other two. 'Lucky you yelled. I forgot to watch the rock.'

'OK,' said Connor. 'Go very carefully along here.'

Tree branches hung down on this side of the river, some of them nearly touching the surface, and Connor made his way between them with difficulty, fighting to prevent the current from sweeping him onwards too fast. He could see Rick now, floating in the water in his orange buoyancy aid. But why hadn't he been carried away downstream like his kayak? Connor edged around another low-hanging tree, and then he saw it: a fine filament of line stretching between the branch and Rick's floating form.

'Watch out!' he called back to the others. 'It's a fishing line.'

He manoeuvred his kayak alongside his leader. 'Rick!' he called, grabbing his shoulder and shaking it gently. 'Rick, can you hear me?'

Rick's face was pale, and Connor went cold when he saw the blood oozing from an evil-looking gash on his forehead. 'We have to get him out of the water right now,' Connor said to the others as they joined him. 'There's no time to lose.'

'But how did it happen?' asked Priya. 'I don't understand.'

'This,' said Connor grimly, pulling his knife out of his pocket and cutting the fishing line. One end of the line sprang back towards the tree and he pulled the fishing hook out of Rick's dry suit.

'That little thing?' said Priya incredulously.

'And that thin line? How could it . . . ?'

'It did,' said Connor. 'Isn't that enough?'

He was surveying the bank as he spoke. Rick had been right: there was a flat area where they could all get out of the river. It was covered with spindly weeds and nettles, but the bank wasn't too high. Even so, he wasn't sure how they were going to drag Rick out of the water.

'We'll have to get in,' Andy said. 'I don't think it's that deep here. Hang onto my kayak while I check.'

Connor grabbed the edge of Andy's cockpit while Andy lowered his paddle into the water. The blade was barely covered. 'You see?' he said. 'We can easily stand up in it.'

'OK,' said Connor. 'I'll get in first. Priya, you keep your kayak there and I'll hold onto it. I'll tie mine to the tree.'

Connor detached the spraydeck from his kayak and brought his boat alongside the bank. He heaved himself out, clumsy in his urgency, and tied a double half-hitch around a small tree. Then he slipped into the water, holding onto

Priya's stern. The riverbed was slippery underfoot, but it was mostly composed of small stones and he found that he could stand up comfortably, despite the tug of the current.

He nodded to Andy, and moments later his friend was in the water beside him, quickly tying his kayak to the tree. They positioned themselves on either side of Rick's head. 'We have to keep his head as still as we can when we lift him out,' Connor said. 'But we *must* get him out whatever happens. Even in the dry suit he's going to get cold.'

They had all laughed at Rick that morning when he'd appeared in his dry suit. 'How come you get to wear one of them,' Abby had complained, 'and we have to kayak in shorts and T-shirts?'

'I'll probably be too warm,' Rick had laughed. 'But then again, chances are I'll be jumping in and out of the river all day to rescue you lot!'

'You will not!' Abby had retorted. 'It's more likely to be the other way round!'

That had only been an hour and a half ago,

Connor thought now as he bent to check Rick's breathing. He tilted Rick's head back carefully. For one terrible moment it seemed as if he wasn't breathing at all, but when he put his cheek by Rick's mouth he felt the breath, faint but regular.

'I'll count to three,' Connor said to Andy. 'Then we'll try and heave his top half onto the bank. Put your hand under his neck, like this. Ready? One . . . two . . . three . . .'

They lifted together, and managed to get Rick's head and shoulders well out of the water, but then struggled to keep them there. Connor felt his feet slipping on the gravel. He moved his hands down to Rick's hip. 'If we can push him far enough onto the bank,' he grunted to Andy, 'then we can get out of the water and pull him the rest of the way. Try to slide him, but gently.'

They moved Rick, centimetre by centimetre, up the bank, until only his ankles and feet still hung in the water. Connor looked round at Priya, who was holding her kayak in position, ready in case anything went wrong. Her face was pale but her jaw was set in a determined line. Beyond her he could see the others waiting on the far side of the river. He gave a thumbs-up to Toby. The situation was very bad, but at least Rick was alive. There had been a moment when he'd thought . . .

Connor immediately put the notion out of his mind and pulled himself out of the water and up onto the bank. With Andy's help he dragged Rick further onto the flat section and began to check carefully to see if he had any other injuries. The dry suit seemed to be intact. There were no scrapes or tears. He thought back to the accident. 'I saw him bang his head,' he said to Andy and Priya. 'Did you see him hurt anything else?'

They both shook their heads. Connor bent to inspect the gash on Rick's temple. It looked nasty and Connor had little doubt that this was why Rick was unconscious. He ran through his first-aid routine in his head. *Danger*. He'd taken care of that, as far as he could. He could do nothing about the danger from the river. *Response*. Well, Rick wasn't responding, but he was breathing. He wished that Toby was here to help him decide what to do, but he'd made the decision to leave him on the other side, so he had to get on with it. First, they'd better put Rick in the recovery position. No. Not yet . . .

'Can you get the plastic sheeting from your bag?' he said to Andy. 'Before we roll him over we should put something on the ground.'

Andy knelt on the bank and reached into the bow of his kayak, pulling out his dry bag and extracting a plastic sheet. They laid it out on the ground next to Rick. Connor bent to check that he was still breathing, then moved the arm nearest him to a right angle. He lifted Rick's other arm over and placed the back of Rick's hand against his cheek. The hand was warm and Connor realized that this was a good sign. He took hold of the knee furthest from him, lifted it and then pulled towards him. Rick rolled easily onto his side, his hand cushioning his face. Connor tilted his chin back gently and adjusted his legs until he was sure that Rick was stable.

'I'm going to cross over and bring the others back,' he said to Priya and Andy. 'They'll be worried, and we should all be together.'

He realized that he was trembling slightly. It was one thing practising the recovery position with your friends in Scout HQ on a Friday night. It was very different when you had to do it for real.

'Connor . . . ?' said Priya hesitantly, her dark eyes anxious. 'Don't you think that I should go? You're the one who knows most about first aid – and I'm not worried about the crossing. I can show them where to go.'

Connor smiled warmly at her. 'Of course. You're right,' he agreed. 'But, Andy, you should get back in your kayak in case anyone gets into difficulties. You can be ready to help, OK?'

Andy nodded agreement and slithered back into his boat while Connor steadied it with one hand. Priya paddled off between the trees while Andy waited in the eddy under the bank.

Connor turned his attention back to Rick. That gash looked very nasty. The sooner Toby was here, the better.

* * *

On the other side of the river, Toby had seen Connor's thumbs-up sign and watched the two boys heave Rick's inert body onto the bank.

'Why did he give us a thumbs-up?' demanded Abby. 'Anyone can see that something terrible has happened.'

'Because he's alive,' replied Toby quietly.

'You mean, you thought . . . ?' Abby suddenly turned two shades paler beneath her tan.

'I think he must be conscious and breathing. I wish I was over there.' Toby looked worried.

'We could go now,' Jay said impatiently. 'Why is Connor waiting so long?'

'He knows what he's doing,' Toby said firmly. 'We wait here.'

'Something's happening.' Abby pointed across the river. 'They're coming back. No, it's just Priya.'

'Why Priya?' asked Jay.

'Because she's the best kayaker,' replied Toby. 'See? Look how easily she paddled across there.'

Less than a minute later, Priya appeared beside them. 'I'm going to help you all over,' she said.

'Rick's safe, but he's unconscious.' Her voice wavered, but she forced herself to continue. 'He's banged his head. Connor needs you to look at it, Toby. You can get across there, can't you? You all can.'

Toby looked at the rushing water. He'd been going backwards and forwards across water like this just yesterday and he'd enjoyed it. But the river was deep now, and getting deeper with every minute that passed, and their Scout Leader was lying unconscious on the opposite bank. They really were on their own, and if anything happened . . .

'OK?' asked Priya again. 'There's no time to waste. Let's move. I'll go across first to show you the route. It's hard work getting up to the crossing. Come on.'

Toby snapped out of his anxious thoughts. There was no choice. He could hardly stay where he was. He followed the other Tigers upstream, paddling hard. When they reached the crossing point, Priya indicated the triangular rock on the far side, then made her way easily across to it.

Abby and then Jay followed her, both of them paddling swiftly and keeping their eyes fixed on the rock. Toby was steeling himself to set out when he saw Priya coming back, smiling at him.

'Don't look so worried,' she told him. 'I thought you were the best of everyone yesterday. Nearly as good as me!'

Toby found himself grinning back at her. He couldn't help himself. They were in a bad spot, but suddenly he was glad he was in it with the Tigers. He watched Priya spin on her axis and send her kayak flashing through the heart of the current. He followed unhesitatingly, paddling furiously as he felt the water rushing underneath the little boat. Spray broke over the side as he turned, focusing hard on the black rock. He joined the others with a quick smile at Priya and she led them along the bank between the trees, back to Andy and Connor.

Andy took hold of the kayaks as they arrived, fastening them quickly to the others but tying their painters through the grablines on top. Toby climbed out and joined Connor on the bank. He pulled on a pair of disposable gloves from his first-aid kit and inspected the cut on Rick's head. 'Being in the water probably stopped it bleeding too much,' he said. 'but it's going to need stitches. Pass me that water bottle, Connor.'

The others watched as Toby poured clean water over the wound. 'Why do you have to do that?' asked Jay. 'It's been under water.'

'This is *clean* water,' Toby said, taking a sterile dressing from the kit and pressing it gently to the wound while he cleaned the surrounding skin carefully. 'The river water looks clean, but it might not be. I'll put a bandage on this for now.'

As Toby bandaged Rick's head, the other Tigers tied up their kayaks and climbed onto the bank. Toby looked up at Connor. 'We have to get help,' he said. 'Rick should go to hospital right now.'

'Look,' exclaimed Jay. 'He's awake!'

Toby turned back to Rick. His eyes were open, but they weren't focused on anything. Toby lowered his head beside Rick's but Rick didn't seem to see him. 'Rick?' he said. 'Can you hear me?'

'Have to call the weather station,' muttered Rick. 'Going on holiday . . . Is the car back from the garage, Sarah? Tired . . .' His voice trailed away and he closed his eyes again.

'I'm going to phone for help,' said Connor. 'Rick's confused. Sarah's his wife. Can you give me the grid reference, Toby?'

'But you can't call anyone,' said Abby in a small voice. 'The phone was in Rick's kayak. And so was most of our food.'

There was a long silence as they stared at each other. It was broken by Connor. 'It's up to us, then,' he said. 'Somehow, we're going to have to get out of this.'

'But there are seven of us,' said Toby, suddenly realizing the full extent of the disaster, 'and only six kayaks.'

CHAPTER 10

'We need to see if we can get away from the river here,' Connor said urgently. 'If we can climb out of this valley, we should be able to find help.'

'We can't around here,' said Toby, who had taken out his map and was inspecting it carefully. 'On this side of the river there's nothing for miles except forest and moorland. There's something that might be a house about four miles away. But it could just be a barn.'

'All the same, we should take a look around,' Connor decided. 'Toby, you go. You can't do any more for Rick just now. Take Abby and Andy with you.'

Connor turned back to check on Rick again. Jay and Priya began hauling the kayaks out of the water. They could all see that the river was still rising, and rising fast.

Toby led the way up a gentle slope between spindly trees, treading carefully to avoid the nettles.

'Maybe there *is* a way out,' Abby said optimistically. 'This doesn't seem too bad.'

'No,' replied Andy, 'but *that* does . . .'

Toby looked ahead and saw a sheer rocky wall rising up in front of him. 'It might be climbable,' said Abby. 'I can see plenty of holds.'

'No way,' said Toby hurriedly. Knowing Abby, she'd be halfway up the cliff before he could stop her if he wasn't careful. 'We're in enough trouble already and I really don't think we could get Rick up there.'

'There might be a gap somewhere,' Andy suggested. 'Let's explore a bit more.' He made his way along the foot of the cliff, then stopped with a yell of pain.

'What is it?' demanded Toby. 'What's happened now?'

Andy turned back. 'It's OK,' he said. 'I stubbed my toe on a tree stump, that's all. Look, there are lots of them. You can't see them properly because of all the nettles and stuff.'

'Well, just be a bit more careful,' said Toby. 'It doesn't look like there's a way up in this direction.'

Andy kept going for a few more metres but they could all hear the sound of the river getting louder, and sure enough, after a few more steps they found themselves looking down into the rushing water.

'This is where the river all gets squashed together,' Toby said, gazing at the torrent. 'At least we've got a good view of it from here.'

'I reckon I could kayak through there,' Abby said. 'We all could, couldn't we?'

'You're forgetting about Rick,' Toby pointed out. 'And the fact that we only have six kayaks.'

'We might have to go for help. It might be the only way.' Abby frowned.

'Let's hope not,' said Toby. 'It's better if we can all stay together. Let's explore in the other direction.'

They retraced their steps carefully and followed the cliff to its northern end. There was no break in it anywhere.

'That's it, then,' said Toby. 'We'd better go back and tell the others.'

'Hey, look,' cried Abby. 'There's a lemonade bottle stuck in that tree.'

The branch in front of her was at about head height. The bottle was tangled in amongst some other debris. With a feeling of dread, Toby began to inspect the other nearby trees. They all had pieces of dead wood and grass clinging to their lower branches. 'Come on,' he said urgently. 'We have to tell Connor.'

'Tell him what?' demanded Abby. 'What are you so worried about?'

'Can't you see?' said Toby. 'All that stuff is up there in the branches because that's how high the river rises. We can't stay here. It's going to be completely underwater before long.' He turned and started crashing through the undergrowth, back towards the river, ignoring the stings on his bare legs.

'Toby, wait,' called Abby. 'I thought I saw . . .'

But Toby ignored her. 'We have to get back to the others,' he shouted as he ran. 'Hurry!'

He arrived back at the riverbank and was astonished to see Rick sitting up. A quick glance at Connor's face, however, told him that all was not well.

'Hello, Ben,' Rick said. 'Have you got the croissants? They sell out if you don't get there early enough. I've got a terrible headache this morning. See if there's any coffee, will you? I think I need to lie down . . .' With that, he subsided onto the plastic sheet and laid his head down on the bundle of clothes that Connor had provided for a pillow.

'He thinks he's in France,' Connor said. 'Ben's one of his children.'

'He's concussed,' Toby explained. 'We'll have to watch him all the time; he could easily be sick or become unconscious again. But, Connor, we *have* to get out of here. This whole patch of ground is going to be underwater soon, and there's no way out. There's a complete ring of cliffs around us.'

'OK,' said Connor. 'I have to think. There must be something we can do . . .'

'Toby?' said Priya suddenly. 'Where are Abby and Andy?'

'I don't believe it . . .' Toby turned round, a frown on his face. 'I told them to follow me.'

'They can't be far away,' Jay reassured him. 'You said it yourself: there's no way out.'

'Except the river,' Connor said, standing up. 'We'd better find them.'

But there was no need. There was a crashing in the undergrowth, and Abby came into sight with Andy close behind her. She was flushed and excited. 'We've found a way to get out of here!' she said, ignoring Connor and Toby's attempts to ask where she'd been. 'You have to come and see.'

'There's no way up those cliffs,' Toby said irritably. 'You know there isn't. We checked every centimetre.'

'Not that,' said Abby impatiently.

'Well, what then?'

'Logs,' she announced triumphantly. 'Big logs. And they're old ones too. They should float really well. Can't you see?' She stared at the blank faces around her. 'We can make a raft! We know how to do it, don't we?'

There was a pause. 'If you think I'm getting on any raft made by you, then you're wrong,' muttered Jay at last.

Abby gave him an angry stare.

'No – wait.' Connor stood up and started pacing backwards and forwards. 'If we had a raft, then Rick could lie on it, maybe. We only have to float down through this fast part and then it's like a normal river. I mean, there aren't any more rapids, are there?'

Toby shook his head slowly from side to side. 'You're right,' he said. 'Once we're past these cliffs we're out of the big hills. It's not that far to the campsite and we can get help.'

'These logs . . .' Connor turned to Abby and Andy. 'How big are they? Can we shift them?'

'We tried lifting one,' Andy told him. 'It wasn't easy, but with lots of us we should be able to manage. They're bigger than the ones we used on the lake. They ought to make a serious raft.'

'Maybe they would,' said Jay. 'But how are we going to fix them together?'

Abby's face fell. 'I never thought of that,' she said.

'It's OK,' exclaimed Toby. 'I've got some rope.'

'But how? Why?' Connor was staring at Toby, who shrugged.

'I saw it lying there and I thought, why not? It's tucked in the bow of my kayak behind my bag. I'll get it.'

Suddenly everyone was laughing. 'You're completely crazy, Toby,' said Priya. 'But I'm glad you are.'

'Why is that crazy?' Toby protested. 'I just thought it would . . .'

'Come in useful!' the Tigers yelled in unison.

'Right,' said Connor. 'One of us has to stay with Rick, but everyone else can help to bring the logs down here.'

'I'll stay here,' Toby said. He was thinking that Priya and Jay had been stuck on the bank waiting for some time now. It would be good for them to have something to do. A quick glance showed him that Connor understood. 'I want to have a good look at the map as well,' he added.

'OK,' said Connor. 'Shout if you need us, Toby. Let's go, everyone.'

Not for the first time, Connor felt very glad that he had Toby as his Assistant Patrol Leader. They had worked together for so long now that they understood one another without the need for words. They both knew how important it was to keep everyone in the patrol active. It meant that they stayed warm and didn't have time to worry about the difficult situation they were in. Connor knew that when Jay had snapped at Abby, it was only because he was worried. And that was fair enough. Connor was worried too.

'You see?' said Abby. 'They're perfect!'

She was standing beside a stack of moss-covered logs. They had clearly been there for some time – the sawn faces were grey and weathered – but a quick check showed Connor that the wood had not rotted. 'They're pine,' he said, looking at the bark and the widely spaced growth rings. 'Or some other kind of softwood. You're right, Abby. They couldn't be better.'

Abby beamed with pleasure and shot a look at Andy. He had his disposable camera in his hand and he took a quick snapshot of the pile of logs.

'Grab the other end of the top one,' Connor said to Jay. 'Remember to bend your knees.'

Jay flashed a look at Connor – then his face broke into a grin. 'Yeah, OK,' he said. 'You're right. I probably would have done it wrong . . . Are you ready – *lift*.'

Connor straightened his knees and felt the weight of the log in his arms. 'I don't know how far I can carry this,' he said. 'Maybe if we have two of you on either side . . .'

Jay worked his way awkwardly around the side of the pile as Connor stepped backwards. As soon as there was room, Abby and Andy positioned themselves on either side and Connor felt some of the strain go from his arms. 'All right, Jay?' he asked, and when the other boy nodded, he began to walk backwards again, with quick glances over his shoulder to see where he was going. Priya ran on ahead, trampling down the nettles and directing Connor onto the best path. The muscles in his arms were burning by the time he reached the riverbank.

'OK,' said Abby. 'Slide it into the water.'

'No, wait,' called Toby. 'We have to make sure it doesn't float away. Bring them all down to the bank first, and then we can put them in the water when we're ready to make the raft.'

'If we don't get them down here fast,' said Connor, 'we won't even have to put them in the water. Look – the river's nearly up to the top of the bank already. We have to hurry.'

They raced back through the spindly trees and brought log after log down to the water's edge. Toby had retrieved the rope from his kayak, and as soon as they had enough logs to begin work, Jay and Andy slipped into the water and began lashing them together.

'We've got plenty of rope here,' said Jay. 'If we leave some spare at the beginning and the end, then we can fasten a kayak on either side. It'll help us steer it.'

'Great idea,' said Connor. The logs floated high on the surface and he nodded with satisfaction as he saw Jay make a neat clove-hitch around the first one, and then another one.

'There is no way I want this coming apart,' Jay said, looking up at Connor and then starting to assemble the raft.

'Won't they get cold in the water?' asked Priya.

'We're lucky,' Connor told her. 'We've had weeks and weeks of hot sun. The river's nowhere near as cold as it could be, and they're working hard. You're right, though. We need to be careful, and we should all eat something. I know most of the food was lost with Rick's kayak, but we've all got snacks and water, haven't we?'

'Connor,' called Toby as the other Tigers searched for snacks in their bags. 'Rick's awake again.'

Connor joined Toby as Rick pushed himself upright, resisting Toby's attempts to keep him down. 'What are they doing?' Rick was staring at Jay and Andy, who had almost finished lashing the logs in place.

'We lost your kayak,' Connor told him, 'so we've made a raft. 'We're going to take you down to the campsite and get help.'

'The water's still rising,' Rick said, his eyes focusing on the river for a moment. 'We'd best raft the kayaks together. It'll be safer that way. You know how to do it. Lay your paddles crosswise. Where's my helmet?'

Rick reached up and felt the bandage encircling his head. 'What's going on?' he demanded, frowning. He winced as if his head was hurting again. 'What's been happening here?'

'You had an accident,' Connor explained. 'You've been unconscious, Rick. You really should rest.'

He saw Rick struggle to say something else, but then his eyes glazed over again and he lay back on one elbow, staring vacantly at the river.

'It's done,' called Jay a short while later. He climbed onto the bank and then hopped onto the raft. It dipped a little with the weight, but it definitely floated.

'OK,' said Connor. 'Fasten your kayak and

mine on either side, Jay, then let's get ready to leave. There's just one thing, though. I don't think we can put Rick on the raft, not the way he is. He might try and stand up or something. I think he'll be safer in a kayak with two of us on either side. So someone will have to go on the raft.'

'Me,' said Priya. 'I'm the lightest . . . Don't look at me like that, Connor. I'll be just as safe on the raft as you will in the kayaks. It's not going to capsize, is it?'

She untied her own kayak, pulled it out of the water, then got in and began adjusting the footrests. 'Rick's not actually going to paddle, is he?' she said. 'I'll set them all the way back. There!' She pulled herself out again. 'And look – the water's level with the bank now. We can get Rick into my kayak on the side here and then slide him into the water.'

'You're right,' Connor said. 'Rick, can you get into this kayak if me and Toby help you?'

Rick slowly stood up with their help and moved over to the kayak. With help from Jay, they managed to get him seated, then Toby gently eased his helmet on over his bandage and fastened the strap. Rick sat in the kayak, looking confused, as Connor explained what they were going to do.

'Andy, Abby and Toby will make a raft of their kayaks, with you in the middle,' he said. 'Me and Jay will be either side of Priya on her raft. We'll all stick together and let the river carry us through, OK?'

Rick didn't seem to register what Connor was saying at all. Connor shrugged, frowning, and Andy, Abby and Toby all got into their kayaks and slid out onto the river. Then Connor pushed Rick out to join them.

Andy and Abby took up position on either side of Rick, laying their paddles across in front of him and taking hold of his cockpit edge. Connor fastened the bows and sterns of the kayaks together using the painters that were neatly coiled under bungee straps on each boat and threading them through the toggles. Toby paddled into place beside Andy, and Connor started to fasten his kayak to the others.

'Don't,' said Toby. 'Better if one of us can move fast. I mean, if something goes wrong . . . Not that it will.'

'OK,' said Connor, getting into his own kayak. 'Good idea.

'Hang onto me,' Toby said to Andy. 'I'll paddle us out into the middle . . .'

Floating in the eddy, they all looked back at the grassy ledge where they'd spent the last hour and a half. Water was lapping at the place where Rick had been lying, and Connor could feel currents beneath the surface of the eddy tugging at his boat.

'Everyone ready?' he asked.

The other Tigers nodded. Connor could see that they were all scared. 'It's frightening,' he said. 'And it's dangerous. But we've done other things that were dangerous. We'll be OK as long as we look out for each other and take care. Kayaks, you go first.'

He watched as the raft of four kayaks, with Rick's bandage flashing white under his helmet

141

in the middle, moved out into the current and shot off downstream.

'All right, Priya?' he asked. Priya's dark eyes glittered with excitement. Connor and Jay dipped their paddles into the water once . . . twice . . . And then the river carried them away.

CHAPTER 11

With his heart in his mouth, Connor watched the kayaks ahead of him being sucked into the swollen water rushing between the two cliffs. Then they vanished from sight round a bend.

'Connor!' cried Jay. 'Paddle!'

'Sorry,' he replied. The raft had started to move more quickly. Priya had taken firm hold of the truncated stub of a branch that stuck up from one of the logs, and now the two boys tried to steer by co-ordinating their paddling. Connor struggled to straighten the raft as it moved out into the river, but although he paddled as hard and fast as he knew how, it began to spin round as it accelerated towards the fastest part of the river. 'Get ready to fend off!' he yelled to Jay over the roar of the tumbling water. 'We can't control this thing. We might bump into the rocks.'

'What can I do?' Priya shouted.

'Stay in the middle and hold on,' Connor called back, setting his jaw and paddling fast. The river swirled them onwards, spinning the raft round and taking it towards the opposite bank. Just as they were about to hit the rocky wall, Connor forced his paddle out sideways and pushed hard. The logs scraped briefly against the rock and a shudder ran through the raft, but then they were away again, Priya clinging tightly to the wood beneath her.

'Look out,' called Jay. 'It's going to get worse.'

They had rounded the bend in the river now, and Connor saw a vast stretch of turbulent white water ahead of them. The huge volume of water coming down the river was being thrown back off one wall of the narrow gorge to crash into water coming in a different direction. He could feel the enormous power of the river through the thin skin of his kayak.

'The raft is strong,' he yelled to Priya as they rapidly approached the white water. 'We might get buffeted a bit, but we'll be OK.'

Priya shot him a quick glance and he knew that she'd seen through the false confidence of his words. But he *had* been on water like this before, when he was only ten years old. He'd been in an inflatable raft on the Colorado river in the United States, with his whole family – though of course it was different when you were on your own in a raft you'd built yourself with an injured leader somewhere up ahead.

'Here we go!' he yelled. 'Hang on!'

The raft suddenly tipped forward as they crossed a massive area of surging water. They all smashed down into a trough, and it was as if a wave had broken over them, but the raft came up again. Water was streaming from Priya's hair, but Connor was amazed to see that she was smiling. The raft spun round again. There was another crashing jolt as it hit the bank, and Jay fended off with his paddle; then they were careering onwards once more, battling through spray and rough water until, quite suddenly, it was over, and they were floating on a wide green river with trees on either side, their roots submerged.

'Over here,' came Toby's voice from away to their right.

Connor glanced over and saw the four kayaks close in to the bank. 'Pull hard,' he called to Jay. 'Let's see if we can steer this thing a bit.'

Jay put his back into paddling and the raft began to move uncertainly towards the river bank. It was almost impossible to keep it going in a straight line, and Connor was aware that even though the river was now wide and flat, the massive quantity of water was moving onwards with immense power. As they neared the waiting kayaks, Abby stretched out a paddle and Connor was just able to grab it as they drifted past.

'Thanks, Abby,' he said. 'Are you all OK?'

'It wasn't too bad,' Toby told him. 'The last bit was the worst.'

'It's a pity we can't go back and do it again,' said Abby. 'It was awesome.'

Connor was about to remind her that they were in a serious situation when he realized that there was a wobble in her voice: she was trying to put on a brave face. 'Well, we're through the worst now,' he said. 'You were amazing, Priya. You looked as if you were actually enjoying yourself.'

'It's a very good raft. I felt completely safe – but Toby's right, that last bit was scary. What happens next?'

'It's about six kilometres to the place where we were planning to camp,' Connor said. 'I don't think there's a phone there, but it won't be too far to a road. Then we can get help.'

Rick hadn't uttered a word since they'd been talking. Now he turned his head and looked at Connor as if he'd never seen him before. 'What's the time?' he asked suddenly. 'I think I have a train to catch.'

'It's OK,' Connor told him. 'Everything's going according to plan. Sit tight in your kayak and we'll get you home.'

'Home . . .' Rick muttered vaguely. 'Yes, I'd like that.'

'Do you think the water is still rising?' asked Andy, who had his camera in his hand once more and was trying to get a shot of all the Tigers with the river in the background. 'Only, I've been watching the trees and it looks like it's gone up about five centimetres while we've been sitting here. Or maybe it's just waves . . .'

'The banks aren't all that high, are they?' Toby murmured thoughtfully. 'You know, it's possible that this might be worse than we thought. What if the whole valley floods?'

Connor looked around. A line of trees marked the usual line of the river bank, but the river had already risen well beyond that and had reached the brambles and gorse bushes growing higher up the bank. It had surged through the narrow gorge, and beyond the far bank Connor could now see a wide, level valley of green pastures dotted with trees. 'You're right,' he said to Toby. 'We should get moving now. Let's make for the campsite and get off the river. It's eleven o'clock. We'll be there in less than an hour.'

'Lunch time' – Abby grinned – 'I'm getting hungry.'

'You can eat as much as you like once we're safe,' Connor told her. 'You and Andy should be able to paddle enough to steer. Toby, you go on your own and lead the way – keep an eye out for any obstacles. This rain might have brought down debris.'

They pushed off from the bank and the river took them once more, carrying them downstream faster than they could have paddled. The raft was still difficult to steer, but they managed to keep it in the middle, avoiding the hazard of over-hanging trees on either side. There was a moment of panic when they suddenly saw an old stone bridge ahead, the water rushing though the arches with very little clearance for their heads, but they were all through before Connor even had time to think that they had just passed under a road where they might have found help.

'We couldn't have stopped even if we'd tried,' Jay pointed out, seeing the look on his face. 'You don't realize how fast you're going until you come to something like that.'

'I know,' said Connor. 'But we were so close.'

'It doesn't matter...' Priya was smiling. 'Look!'

Ahead of them, Toby was pointing with his

paddle. Above the trees the Scout flag was fluttering, with the 6th Matfield's own flag below it.

'We've made it,' cried Priya. 'Brilliant, Connor!'

'We need to get over to that side of the river,' Jay called urgently.

Connor realized that he was right. The flag was still some distance away, but the river was moving so fast . . . 'Paddle hard,' he yelled.

But his words were in vain. As they drew near to the flag, the raft was caught in a strong, swirling current that dragged it inexorably towards the other bank. And then a gap in the trees opened up and they saw the campsite. The flagpole rose straight up from the middle of a broad sheet of water that stretched on into the distance between the tree trunks. The river had burst its banks here, and as the current carried them onwards, Connor had a brief glimpse of flooded fields, and hedges surrounding nothing but water.

* * *

Toby swung his kayak round to get a better look at the campsite. Paddling hard against the current, he was just able to hold his position. Rick hadn't told them much about the place beyond explaining that there were some woods where they would be building shelters. He could see them now, the trees rising straight out of the water. No chance of camping there, even if they could have landed. He'd half hoped there might be someone there. They could have yelled a message . . .

But there was no one, and the three kayaks that were rafted together were drifting quickly away from him. He remembered guiltily that he was supposed to be leading the way. He turned his kayak round and paddled fast to catch up with Abby and Andy. When he reached them, he found himself fixed by Rick's blue eyes. They were focused now.

'No chance of stopping there, then,' he said.

'You're better,' Toby said, feeling relief wash over him. 'That's great!'

'I'm alive,' Rick murmured, 'thanks to you lot.

But I don't feel right. I've got a terrible headache. The sooner we get off this river and find help, the better.'

'Yes,' said Toby. 'We thought the campsite—'

'I saw it,' Rick interrupted. 'Listen, Toby, if you spot a place to stop, then do it. They'll be looking for us by now, so try and stay in the open. Oh . . .' He gave a sudden groan and clutched at his head. Then he went very pale and his eyes glazed over again.

Andy and Abby looked at Toby with alarm on their faces.

'I'm going on ahead,' he said. 'When I find somewhere, I'll signal. I'll tell the others what I'm doing.'

He pressed on, quickly catching up with the raft, which was drifting along a hundred metres ahead. 'I don't like it,' he said, grabbing hold of Connor's kayak. 'Rick's OK one minute, but then, the next, he looks terrible. I'm going to try and find somewhere to stop, OK?'

'Sure – but remember, this thing is almost impossible to steer. We need plenty of warning

. . . And be careful, Toby,' he called after him as he paddled away.

Toby wished he could remember more of the detail from the map. Pretty soon they'd be off the one he'd brought anyway, but he'd looked at maps of the whole river before they set out. There must be places where they could get off the water and climb up to higher ground. However, the situation didn't look promising, and he knew that in a few miles this river converged with a much bigger one. That was OK, because it meant that there were bound to be more people. There was a town a short distance down the bigger river, but there were also weirs, and maybe other dangers too.

As Toby paddled, he gazed out over flooded meadows. It seemed impossible that this could have happened so fast. And then he caught sight of something on the other bank – a wooden jetty still standing clear of the water, and beyond it a broad grassy slope leading up to a small house. He yelled out to the others, lifted his paddle to point – and felt a sudden stinging pain as a branch slashed across his face. Before he could react, the branch had lodged in his buoyancy aid and the power of the current was pulling his kayak away from him. The spraydeck was ripped from the cockpit, and Toby tried to grab the kayak with his feet as he thrashed around in the water, but he couldn't hold on, and then the kayak was gone, drifting away towards the opposite bank.

CHAPTER 12

Toby looked desperately after the vanishing kayak. How could he have been so *stupid*? He was the one who was supposed to be the lookout. He discovered that he was clinging with both hands to the branch that had ensnared him. His head and shoulders were out of the water, but the current was tugging at his body with ferocious power and the branch was bending alarmingly. It wasn't very thick and was being bent to breaking point. There was a sudden *crack!* and he saw that the wood was splitting, white showing through the fractured bark.

'Help!' he yelled. '*Help! Quick!* It's going to *break.*'

Back on the raft, Priya had seen the accident happening and had immediately started to untie Jay's kayak. Now, Toby twisted round and saw Jay paddling at top speed up the river. At first he couldn't work out why he was going in totally the wrong direction and he almost called out again; then he realized that Jay was going to cross upstream and let the current bring him down to where Toby was hanging onto the branch. He saw the group of three kayaks speed by on the other side of the river, and had a glimpse of Abby's worried face as she called out to him to hold on. Then the raft came past.

'Any moment now,' Connor shouted to him. 'You'll have to grab hold of Jay's kayak and he'll tow you to the raft. We'll stop as soon as we can.'

There was another splitting noise from the branch and Toby felt it starting to give. He looked around desperately for something to grab hold of, but there was nothing. If Jay didn't arrive soon, he would be swept away by the river.

Jay had started to paddle across. His kayak was whipped round by the current, and now he was approaching fast. There was a final *crack!* and the branch snapped off. Toby's head went under the water for a second, then he was up, floating on his back, searching for Jay's kayak.

He heard a yell, but in his confusion he couldn't tell where it had come from. 'Toby! I'm here! Grab hold!'

He lifted his arms out of the water and saw a flash of blue. He reached out, grabbed for the stern of the kayak, and missed, gulping down a mouthful of water that made him gag.

'Take it easy,' Jay told him. 'I'm right beside you. Watch out for my paddle.'

Toby kicked hard with his legs, and suddenly bumped into the side of Jay's boat.

'Cool,' said Jay. 'Grab the stern. I'll tow you over to the raft.'

Toby was trembling, taking in great gulps of air. His heart was beating like a machine gun. 'I thought I'd had it . . .' His voice was little more than a croak.

'No way.' Jay shook his head firmly. 'We're the Survival Squad, right? We'll make it through this together.'

'Thanks,' said Toby. 'Thanks for rescuing me.'

'I haven't done it yet,' grunted Jay. 'Stop

talking and let me paddle.'

He turned away and Toby felt the kayak surge forward as Jay pulled even harder on the paddles. They drew ever closer to the raft, and then he saw Priya's dark eyes watching them anxiously until they finally drew alongside. She reached out a hand to help him heave himself onto the raft. 'Are you OK?' she demanded anxiously.

'I'm fine,' Toby gasped, coughing. 'I swallowed a bit of water, that's all. Are you sure this raft will support both of us?'

'It'll have to,' said Connor grimly. 'Move—'

'Look,' cried Priya, who was starting to re-fasten Jay's boat to the raft. 'It's your kayak, Toby.'

The river was now entering a wooded stretch and they could see Toby's kayak, caught amongst a tangle of branches.

'I'll go,' said Jay, but Connor stopped him.

'Carry on, Priya,' he said. 'The others have seen it too. That's calm water over there. I reckon we can reach it with the raft if we paddle hard. Then we can take a rest and check on Rick.'

Connor called out to Andy and signalled that

they should all meet by the kayak; then he and Jay manoeuvred the unwieldy raft towards the eddy where Toby's kayak was bobbing gently.

Toby watched what Connor was doing carefully. 'You're trying to use the current,' he said, impressed.

'Right,' grunted Connor. 'You can see the way the surface is moving. If you get the right bit, it takes you where you want to go. If you get the wrong bit, there's not much you can do about it. We've found that out the hard way. There – look!'

The current pulled them in towards the side of the river, and then they were moving slowly upstream. With a couple of quick strokes, Connor brought them to rest beside Toby's kayak.

'I thought I was never going to see it again,' said Toby, reaching out to grab his boat.

'You're lucky you did,' replied Connor as Andy and Abby steered their little group of kayaks into the quiet water under the trees.

Looking around at his friends, Toby could see a mixture of relief and tiredness on their faces.

Then he saw Rick, his face pale beneath the bandage, and he realized that Andy and Abby were helping him to sit upright. His eyes were open, but they weren't focusing properly.

'What are we going to do?' asked Priya.

'I wish we could have stopped where that road crossed over the river,' said Connor.

'And there was that house . . .' said Abby.

'We'll just have to keep going until we do find help,' Toby said. 'I know it looks bad right now, but it's better than waiting here. We shouldn't stay too long beneath these trees either. Remember what Rick said: they're bound to start looking for us soon and they won't see us under here.'

'We'll move on in a minute,' said Connor reluctantly. He had been checking Rick's pulse and breathing and he was still very worried. 'I don't think we have any choice. But right now we have to eat and drink. Has anyone got any food left?'

Toby glanced around at the others: it was clear that they'd already eaten everything they had.

'Just as well we found my kayak then,' he said with a grin. He crawled across the raft and pulled out his oversized bag. 'I always put in a bit extra, just in case.'

He pulled out a carefully sealed polythene bag and unwrapped it to reveal a collection of energy bars. 'Thanks, Toby.' For once, Abby was too tired to make fun of him. They all ate the bars and drank from their water bottles.

The heavy cloud that had blanketed the sky since dawn was breaking up above the trees and hot sun crept through the overhanging branches. 'Just as well,' said Connor, looking up. 'I was worried about you getting cold, Toby. And Rick too.'

'Let's push on,' Toby said, slipping gratefully back into his kayak. 'We're bound to find help soon.'

Connor could tell that the others were all fighting against tiredness; that could be very dangerous. But he was even more worried about Rick. He knew perfectly well that if he'd banged his head like that at home he would have been taken straight to hospital and kept in while the doctors checked him out.

As they steered the raft back out into the river, Priya seemed to be reading his mind. 'At least he's got that dry suit on. He's not cold, is he?' she asked.

'You're right,' said Connor, looking back anxiously to see Abby and Andy following behind the raft. 'But we really do need to find help soon.'

'I know.' She nodded. 'I feel bad, just sitting on the raft like this. I wish I could help to— What's that?'

'What?' asked Connor. 'I can't hear anything.'

'Stop paddling,' said Priya urgently. 'Listen!'

Suddenly Connor heard it – a low throbbing sound somewhere in the distance, back towards the hills.

'It's a helicopter,' called Andy. 'I'd know that sound anywhere.'

Andy and Abby had helped with a helicopter rescue in the Alps when they had gone skiing with their parents after Christmas. Later, all the Tigers had been involved in a rescue that had ended with Andy actually going for a flight in a helicopter when Matfield was cut off by the snow.

'It's getting louder,' cried Abby. 'I think it's coming this way!'

'Paddle!' yelled Connor. 'Paddle as fast as you can. They'll never see us under here.'

Tall trees lined the river and the branches met above their heads. It was like a tunnel that went on for several hundred metres. Up ahead, Connor could see blue sky and sunlight dancing on the surface of the water. If they could only get there in time . . .

The Scouts paddled frantically as the throbbing became a clattering roar, and they saw a brief flash of orange as the helicopter passed directly over their heads. Connor found himself yelling at the top of his voice, and all the others were too.

The clatter faded away for a moment; then, as Connor held his breath, it rapidly grew louder again. 'It's coming back,' he yelled. 'Paddle like crazy! We have to get out of these trees.'

The helicopter was definitely returning, but far more slowly this time, following the course of the river. Connor redoubled his efforts. His arms were on fire. They approached the open water to see the treetops ahead of them tossing to and fro in the downdraught from the helicopter's rotors; but as it passed over their heads the overhanging branches seemed to crowd in thicker than ever. The noise grew to a crescendo, then faded rapidly away upstream.

The Tigers all stopped paddling and stared at each other as they drifted with the current. Seconds later they were clear of the trees, and as they gazed across the waterlogged landscape they spotted the helicopter again, looking like an angry orange fly, disappearing into the distance.

'It might come back,' said Priya hopefully.

'We don't even know if it was looking for us,' Jay pointed out. 'They might think it's very unlikely we could have come this far. They've got miles of river to search.'

The river had widened, and from the trees and bushes poking through the floodwater and marking the bank, they could see that this wasn't just because of the floods. Andy and Abby brought their kayaks in close beside the raft and Andy grabbed hold of Jay's boat.

'I think there are some buildings up ahead,' he said. 'We're going to be OK.'

There was a ragged cheer from the other Tigers, but Connor was looking doubtfully at the low white buildings that had just come into sight. And there was a sign now; a big white sign with huge red letters on it:

DANGER:

WEIR

Toby was ahead of them. He'd seen the sign at the same moment as Connor and he'd turned his kayak, trying to paddle away from the weir. Connor could hear the noise now. He couldn't understand why he hadn't noticed it sooner. After everything else that had happened, this was too much.

'We'll never get away from it,' Jay yelled over the roar. 'The current's too strong. Look at Toby!'

Toby was paddling hard, but his kayak was being swept inexorably past the danger sign. They were catching him, but not fast enough. Andy was still holding onto the raft.

Connor forced himself to think. The weir ahead of them was a straight line across the river. He could see nothing beyond the point where the water poured over the edge, but the noise told him that it was going to be rough. 'Hold onto each other,' he yelled. 'Lay your paddle across the raft, Jay. Priya, lie down flat and hang on tight.'

Priya moved quickly into position while Connor looked along the line of Tigers.

'Toby's going over,' Jay said, his voice shaking with fear.

They all watched in silence. This time there was nothing they could do to help him. He had turned his kayak so that he was facing forward and was paddling fast towards the weir. Connor saw with grim satisfaction that he was putting everything he'd learned into practice. Watching him paddle purposefully towards the weir, no one would ever have known that he was deliberately heading into an unknown danger. He reached the weir, still paddling hard – and then he was gone.

'Now it's our turn,' yelled Connor, looking round at the set jaws and pale faces of the other Tigers. 'Hold on, everyone. We're going to be OK!'

The raft was close to the edge now, and the noise was terrible. Five metres . . two metres . . .

They went over the edge, and the world exploded into a confusion of noise and foam.

CHAPTER 13

For several long moments the raft and the kayaks were under water. As they came to the surface again, Connor just had time to yell, 'Hang on!' before another wall of water hit them and sent them lurching sideways. All around them was a tumbling, foaming confusion of water and spray. Connor glanced to either side and saw that all the Tigers were still clinging firmly to paddles and kayaks. Then his eyes caught Priya's.

She lay stretched out on the raft, holding onto the rope ends, and her eyes were shining. 'We did it, Connor!' she yelled.

Even as she said the words, Connor could feel the turbulence lessening beneath the thin skin of his kayak. Then he remembered Toby. He couldn't see him anywhere, and his stomach lurched. 'Look for Toby!' he shouted to the others.

They had emerged from the white water into a smooth-flowing section of river. Connor looked back over the wild chaos they'd just crossed, expecting to see Toby's kayak spinning upside down in the water. But there was no sign of him.

'There!' cried Abby, almost sobbing with relief. 'There he is! He's up ahead!'

Connor followed her pointing arm, saw a flash of blue and a red helmet, and felt his eyes misting with tears. He wiped them away with his sleeve. Toby was facing them and paddling hard, but the river was still sweeping him backwards. 'I didn't fall in that time,' he called to them, his face split by a huge grin. 'I saw you come over. It was awesome.'

'I'd do it again,' said Priya.

Suddenly all the Tigers were talking loudly, laughing and yelling to each other. It was almost as if they'd forgotten that they were still drifting down a flooded river with a badly injured Scout Leader.

'Shut up, all of you,' Connor yelled suddenly. 'We're still in danger. Look at that!'

The river had widened, and now they saw a huge area of churning water ahead. 'It's the other river,' called Toby. 'The big one. I showed you on the map, remember?'

'Let's make for the other bank,' Connor said. 'There's so much water in this river, the current is pushing right across to the other side – look, I think I can see a sort of beach, and there's higher ground behind it. If we manage to land, we can get help. Get ready . . .'

The current hurled them out into the larger river, and suddenly water stretched away on every side, brown and yellow with the mud that had been brought downstream.

'We can't steer like this,' Jay yelled as the unwieldy collection of kayaks and raft was spun round in the churning water. 'Look, we're going to miss the landing place.'

Ahead of them, Toby had navigated the rough water expertly in his kayak, and was now approaching the narrow stony beach on the far bank. But Connor could see that the current was going to carry the rest of them past a small rocky promontory and out into the river again if they didn't do something urgently.

'You're right,' he told Jay. 'Andy, can you and Abby make it with Rick?' With a jolt, he realized that he'd barely given a thought to their injured leader. As they'd gone over the weir, Rick had sat slumped, glassy-eyed, in his kayak; now, when Connor glanced at him again, he was startled to see Rick looking back at him.

'Don't worry about me, Connor,' he said. 'I've got hold of both their kayaks.'

'All right,' said Abby. 'Let's go for it. See you on the shore.' With that, she pushed her kayak away from Jay's, and the raft of three boats drifted free. She and Andy paddled furiously, taking Rick's kayak with them towards where Toby was waiting.

As soon as he and Jay began to paddle the log raft, Connor knew that they weren't going to make it. The light, manoeuvrable kayaks had veered away from them and were moving quickly towards the shore, but the raft was caught in an eddying current that curved deceptively in towards the bank and then slid off past the rocky point. The raft was heavy and sluggish in the water, resisting all their efforts to shift it off its course. They came in close beside the bank, and Connor heard a yell from above him. He looked up and saw Toby racing along a grassy slope beneath the trees. He was holding a paddle and he jumped down from the bank, knee-deep in the water, stretching the paddle towards them.

The red tip was just centimetres away. Priya reached out a long brown arm; she was almost touching it . . . And then the current spun them away again.

'We could swim for it.' Jay was still paddling desperately as the raft drifted towards the rocky outcrop that was their last chance of safety before they were carried away down the swirling river.

'No way,' replied Connor. 'We're going to make it. When I give the word, we paddle harder than we've ever paddled in our lives, OK?'

Jay nodded, his jaw set and his stocky form bent forward in his kayak. Priya moved to the front of the raft.

'What are you doing?' Connor cried.

'If there's anything to grab, I want to be ready,' she replied. 'I have to do *something*.'

OK.' Connor watched the current carefully as the headland approached. 'Now – paddle! Go for it!'

At first he thought that their efforts weren't making any difference. The bank was sliding by too fast. But then he realized that it was a little nearer than it had been.

'Go on!' yelled Priya. 'You can do it!'

Connor could now see exactly where the land ended. There was a small line of rocks running out into the water. Beyond, the broad, glinting river stretched to a width of several hundred metres. The thought of himself and Jay and Priya drifting out onto that huge expanse of unknown water was too much. They *had* to make it, he told himself fiercely. He glanced across at Jay and their eyes met for a moment. He saw that Jay was afraid too. 'Paddle!' he yelled again, but as he tried to pull the raft further towards the bank, he felt the strength leaving his arms. *It's no good*, he thought. *We'll never do it . . .*

And then he saw a small, dark, wiry figure waving madly and screaming at them. Toby ran out along the line of rocks, slipped, and fell full length before picking himself up and splashing out through the water to the very tip of the promontory. Once again, he held a paddle out across the water – and this time Priya reached out and took hold of the blade.

Instantly, the raft spun round and Connor's kayak crashed against the rocks. Priya tumbled towards him, but somehow she managed to keep hold of the paddle. The current took hold of the raft again and tried to pull it away from the rocks, but Connor pushed himself out of his kayak and flopped into the water. 'Hang on, Jay,' he called, trying to get a purchase on the slippery rock beneath his feet as the current tugged at his legs.

Priya was safely on the rocks now. Toby, blood streaming from a cut on his leg, pushed the paddle out to Jay, who grabbed hold of it gratefully. 'Get out of the boat,' Toby called. 'Quickly!'

Jay pushed himself upright and half fell into

the water, hanging grimly onto the paddle. As he did so, the raft, with the two kayaks still lashed to either side, was seized by the current and floated quickly out of reach. 'It's OK,' Connor said to a horrified Priya. 'We're safe now. We don't need them any more. We're on dry land.'

Suddenly Priya burst into tears.

Toby stood watching the raft for a moment as it drifted rapidly out of sight. He was panting, and his heart was thumping wildly. A shiver ran down his spine as he pictured what might have been – the raft drifting away with Priya on it, and Connor and Jay with her.

'Thanks, Toby,' said Connor, putting a hand on his shoulder.

'Now we're even.' Jay grinned at Toby. 'I saved you and you saved me.'

'But what about the others?' asked Priya anxiously.

'They're OK, I think,' Toby said. 'I saw them land and then I ran after you lot. I thought you weren't going to make it.'

'Well, we did,' said Connor. 'And now we'd better find the others and see to that cut, Toby.'

With Toby and Priya in the lead, they made their way wearily back along the bank through lush green undergrowth. Toby tried to pick a path between the worst of the nettles, but he heard frequent shouts of annoyance from behind him. He realized that his skin was already burning with stings. He hadn't even noticed the nettles while he'd been chasing madly after the escaping raft.

They rounded a thick patch of brambles and found Abby, Andy and Rick sitting in a grassy clearing. Abby and Andy jumped to their feet and ran towards them, their faces drawn and pale.

'You're all right,' breathed Abby. 'We thought you were . . .'

'We're OK,' replied Connor. 'All of us, thanks to Toby. How's Rick?'

'Not good.' Andy glanced over to their Scout Leader, who was humming to himself and throwing pebbles into the water. 'He thinks he's on holiday in France again.'

Rick looked up at them, his face showing

childish excitement. 'Ah, you're back!' he said. 'That's good. It's time we had lunch. Let's go to the café.' He started to get to his feet, then swayed and put a hand to his head. A look of surprise crossed his face, and Abby rushed over and gently helped him to sit down again.

'You see?' said Andy. 'He should be in hospital.'

Toby could see that the Tigers were all exhausted. 'It doesn't look as if there's anyone living near here. We'll take a look around,' he said, 'but first we should light a fire to get ourselves properly warm, and we need something to eat.'

'Yeah, right!' said Jay. 'We ate all our food, remember. And yours too.'

'Well, it's a good job you rescued my boat.' Toby reached into the bulkhead and pulled out his bag.

'We were only supposed to pack essential items,' Connor said as he opened a small red bag and took out the flint and steel he'd bought from an outdoor shop before the holidays. 'What is that, anyway?'

Toby struck the steel on the flint and the eyes of the other Tigers widened as they saw the small shower of blue sparks. 'I've got some waterproof matches too. But I'd like to try this.'

Connor grinned at him. 'Trust you,' he said. 'Abby and Andy, you go and find wood. Priya and Jay, get some stones and make a fireplace over there.' He pointed to a spot that was clear of the overhanging trees.

As the others got busy, Toby searched around and found some very dry sticks under a pine tree higher up the bank. He collected an armful together, making sure he had enough to get a decent fire going, then carried them down to the fireplace. 'Can I borrow your knife?' he asked Connor.

'You've got your own, haven't you?'

'I know. But I can never get it as sharp as yours. I need really fine shavings for this.'

Connor took the old Swiss Army knife out of his pocket. It had already helped the Tigers in a variety of dangerous situations, and it had helped Connor's dad and grandpa before that. Toby took it with a nod of thanks and began shaving very fine strips of wood off one of the sticks. 'Here,' he said to Connor, when he had made enough for a small ball. 'Hold this. That's right.'

Connor stood with the ball of shavings cupped in his hands and Toby struck the flint with the steel. Sparks flew, but none of them caught. He tried again, and there was a tiny orange glow in the middle of the shavings. 'Quick – blow on it!'

A thin stream of smoke rose from the bundle of shavings, and suddenly the glow was brighter and there was a tiny flicker of flame.

'Put it down,' said Toby. 'That's it.' He took the bigger shavings he'd prepared and added them carefully to the little fire. Before long a small blaze was crackling away. Priya and Jay were bringing Rick to sit beside the fire, and Connor was wondering who he should send to look for help, when there was a crashing of footsteps from the nearby trees and Abby and Andy burst into the clearing, their arms full of wood.

'You're not going to believe this,' Abby said, dumping the wood on the ground with a clatter. 'We're not on the shore at all. We're on an island!'

'So we're as far from help as ever,' added Andy. 'And now we've lost two more kayaks, and we haven't even got the raft.'

CHAPTER 14

'Are you sure?' said Connor. He suddenly felt incredibly tired. 'I mean, *really* sure?'

'Of course we are,' replied Abby. 'We walked all the way round it. And it's a good job it's so high out of the water, because the river's still rising and the current is incredibly fast. I wouldn't want to try and kayak across. I can't believe we ever managed to land here.'

Connor stood up and looked out at the river. Abby was right. Even if they weren't so tired, it would be madness for any of them to try to cross to the shore. He said so now.

'So what are we going to do?' asked Jay. 'We've got nothing to eat and Rick needs to go to hospital.'

Connor looked across at Rick, who lifted an arm in a kind of wave.

'Don't worry about me,' he said, then frowned and rubbed his bandaged head. 'If it wasn't for this headache I'd be fine. I'm warm and I haven't broken anything. I'm just a bit tired, that's all.'

Connor wasn't so sure. He knew they would have to keep a careful eye on Rick, whatever they decided to do. 'How much water have we got?' he asked the others. All their bottles were nearly empty.

'It doesn't matter though,' Jay pointed out. 'There's a million tons of water right there.'

'Flood water gets contaminated,' Connor replied. 'I suppose we've got the tablets, and we could boil it too, but . . .'

'Wait,' said Toby, who had a good fire going now, and was attending to the cut on his knee. 'I just remembered . . . When I was running along the shore, I saw a stream coming down off the rocks. That must mean—'

'There's a spring on the island!' Priya said excitedly, turning to the others. 'He's right! And it's only a little island so it can't be far away. If we find where the stream starts, we'll have

182

fresh water. Right, Toby? I'll go and look.'

'Not on your own,' Connor warned. 'We really don't want any more accidents. Jay, you go with her.'

'So we're going to stay here on the island?' he asked, getting up reluctantly.

'I don't think there's anything else we *can* do,' Connor replied; then he saw that Abby's forehead had creased into a worried frown.

'I just had an awful thought,' she said. 'What if they find the kayaks and think the worst? They might think we've all drowned.'

A chill ran down Connor's spine as he thought of his dad, back at the campsite, and his mum and his sister Ellie waiting at home. All their parents would be going crazy with worry – and their friends. Suddenly, for no reason, he found himself thinking about the Sea Scouts; they'd only just got to know them, but he could picture Sam's laughing face. His head was spinning.

'There's another thing,' said Toby. 'We've come a long way. They may not even be looking for us here. The search is probably going on way back up the river. And if they *do* come this way, how will they know we're here?'

'They'll see the smoke from our fire,' Connor said, looking up at the slender column rising into the sky through the trees and trying to clear his head. 'If they do, they're bound to investigate. With any luck we'll be rescued quite soon.'

But even as Connor said the words, and Jay and Priya went off to look for water, he didn't quite believe them. He looked over to where Toby was delving in his bags once more.

'What now?' asked Abby.

Toby came up with another orange stuff-sack in his hands, from which he removed a small billycan full of sealed packages. 'Emergency rations.' He grinned. 'I thought, you know, if there was a total disaster, we might need them. And this *is* kind of a disaster, isn't it? There's soup and hot chocolate. I think there's enough for everyone.'

They all burst out laughing, and even Rick managed to raise a weak smile. 'I told you – strictly *one* bag only,' he said.

'We're supposed to be prepared, aren't we?' asked Toby as Jay and Priya returned triumphantly with full water bottles and demanded to know what the joke was.

'No joke,' said Connor with a weary smile. 'Just Toby bringing tons of extra stuff as usual.'

'We were going to bivouac in the woods,' Rick told his patrol. 'We were going to cook rabbit.'

'Well, actually,' said Toby, 'I thought we could go fishing. Just in case we don't get rescued tonight.'

'Fishing!' the others exclaimed.

'How are we going to do that?' asked Jay.

'I saved the fish-hook that caught on Rick's jacket,' said Toby, producing it from his pocket. 'And I cut the fishing line from the tree. I thought it was a waste to leave it there, and anyway, it didn't belong there. I was just tidying up.'

'Do you actually know anything about fishing?' Priya wondered.

'Only what I've read in books,' he replied. 'We cut a pole from the wood, tie on the line, and fix a worm to the hook. All we have to do is find some worms – it's simple. Look, the water's boiling. Who'd like some soup?'

When the soup was finished, Connor sent the other Tigers off to look for worms.

'That's good,' said Rick when his Patrol Leader had put two more logs on the fire and came over to sit beside him. 'You have to keep them busy, Connor, especially the younger ones, Jay and Priya . . .' He paused, wincing with pain.

'Isn't there something I can do?' asked Connor anxiously. 'There's some paracetamol in the first-aid kit, but I wasn't sure . . .'

Rick nodded. 'It might help,' he said. 'Like I told you, I don't think I've broken anything. I won't need an operation. And maybe I could have some of that hot chocolate.'

Connor was doubtful, but he told himself that Rick knew much more about first aid than he did. He fetched the painkillers and made Rick a drink, and he was relieved to see some colour returning to the Scout Leader's pale face as he sipped the hot chocolate.

Just then, Connor heard the low drone of a helicopter again. He put down the billycan with a clatter, upsetting what was left of the water, and ran down to the shore. The helicopter was an orange speck, low down to the north. Connor rushed back into the clearing and flung some grass and nettles onto the flames. Smoke rose into the sky, but the throb of the helicopter faded into the distance and died away. The other Tigers came running into the clearing, their faces hopeful, but Connor shook his head.

'It looks as if Toby was right. They're not searching right down here. We may have to wait.'

'But what about Rick?' asked Priya.

'I'll survive, Priya, thanks to you lot,' Rick said. 'Just as long as this headache goes away. Did you find any worms? There is a bright side to all this, you know. It'll count towards your Survival Badge, and you can make a start on your Angling Badge too.'

'I don't really care about badges right now,' said Abby, who was holding several wriggling pink worms in her cupped hands. 'But I wouldn't mind some fish. Soup isn't like real food, is it?'

Toby had been busy fastening the fishing line to the end of the whippy ash pole he had cut in the wood. 'I've used a round turn and two half-hitches,' he told the watching Tigers, 'and then I've tied another one, just to be on the safe side. There . . .' He gave the knot a tug to check it was secure. 'I'll tie the hook on in the same way,' he muttered. 'Ouch! That's sharp.' He looked down at the bead of blood that had appeared on his thumb, then sucked it as the other Tigers laughed.

He ignored them and concentrated on the fiddly job of tying the hook onto the line. He passed the end of the line through the eye of the hook, trying to remember how to make a clinch knot. Next he looped the end four times around the line and then passed it back down through all the loops and pulled it tight. It looked neat and strong.

'Let me see,' said Rick from his seat against the tree.

Toby took the rod and line over to him and Rick examined it carefully. 'So this is what yanked me out of my boat . . .' He turned it over in his hand and tested the strength of the line, then shook his head ruefully. 'I don't remember a thing about it,' he said. 'It's probably just as well. I didn't know you were an angler, Toby. That's just how a fisherman would tie the hook.'

'I know,' said Toby. 'I thought we might be doing some fishing, so I got a book out of the library.'

'Can't we start fishing?' asked Abby. 'It takes ages to catch fish, doesn't it?'

'Go on, Toby,' said Rick with a smile. 'I expect you're an expert at that too.'

Toby took the rod. He felt himself blushing slightly. 'You go first, Abby,' he said, handing it to her.

She fastened a small worm to the hook.

'Isn't that cruel?' asked Andy, wincing as he saw what Abby was doing.

'Well, we could just put the hook in the water

without the worm,' Abby told him. 'But I don't suppose we'd catch anything.'

'We might, actually,' said Toby. 'But worms are better.'

'Anyway, I've done it now,' Abby said. 'Here goes.'

She went down to the bank and held the pole out over the water, dangling the hook just below the surface where the current instantly pulled it off to one side. 'I don't know what to do,' she said, turning back to the others. 'Should I— Oh!'

Toby saw the line suddenly change direction and head upstream. 'You've got something!' he exclaimed. 'I don't believe it!'

The rod jerked in Abby's hands as the fish reached the end of the line. It turned and headed out into the river, then stopped again.

'If you had a reel, you could let it run for a bit and tire itself out,' said Jay. 'Maybe you should just try and pull it in. You could walk backwards.'

'Good idea,' said Toby. 'Go on, Abby. We'll try and grab it when it comes out of the water.'

Then, all at once, the fish was there, wriggling

and flapping on the end of the line as Abby pulled it onto the stony beach. They all stood there for a moment, frozen in astonishment, before Priya pushed Jay out of the way and ran forward to grab the fish in both hands and bang its head efficiently on a rock.

'There,' she said, extracting the hook from the fish's mouth and holding it out, gleaming and silvery. 'We've got some supper. All we have to do now is catch a few more.'

'That was so cool, the way you did that,' said Connor. 'I never thought about having to kill it.'

'I've seen my auntie kill chickens in India,' Priya told him. 'It's not a big deal.'

As the other Tigers argued about who should have the next go with the fishing rod, Toby took Connor to one side. 'I've been thinking,' he said. 'Maybe we should put up some shelters. We could be stuck here tonight.'

Connor nodded. 'I was thinking the same thing,' he said. 'It's all right now, while the sun's shining, but when it gets dark it'll be colder, and it could easily rain again. There are lots of young trees. I reckon we can easily make lean-tos with the tarps.'

They approached the others and explained what they were going to do. 'You mean . . . we're going to be here all night?' said Priya.

Toby cast an anxious look her way. He knew that Priya had worried about being out in the dark before their last adventure in the Welsh hills.

But he needn't have worried. She grinned back at him, her dark eyes shining. 'Cool,' she said. 'We've had plenty of practice and now we're doing it for real.'

CHAPTER 15

'Luckily, we don't need a shelter each,' Connor said. 'We've still got four plastic sheets in the kayaks and we can share shelters to keep warm. We'll make one for Rick close to the fire. We can use those trees there. Abby and Priya, you go together, and Toby and Jay. I'll make one for me and Andy. It looks like he might be a while.'

Andy was fishing, but he wasn't having Abby's luck. 'You were never going to be as good as me,' Abby told him, but he just laughed.

'When I *do* catch one, it'll be twice the size of yours,' he said.

The site was excellent, thought Connor. They'd been so lucky to end up in such a good spot. The ground sloped gently so that any rain would run off, and though there were plenty of trees, none were so big that branches might come crashing down on them in a high wind.

The lightweight plastic tarps that Rick had given them had metal-ringed holes at intervals along the edges, and wrapped up in the middle they found a coil of strong, thin cord and some lightweight tent-pegs. Connor found two suitable saplings and used short lengths of cord to fasten the sheet to them. Another tree provided an anchor point for one corner of the tarp, but he had to cut an ash pole from a nearby thicket and hammer it into the ground with a large stone from the beach to fasten the final corner. Satisfied, he anchored the tarp to the ground with tent-pegs.

'Good work, Connor.'

Connor turned and saw Rick's blue eyes looking up at him. He'd been sleeping fitfully, but now he'd raised himself up on one arm to look around the clearing. 'You're not expecting rescue any time soon, then?'

Connor shook his head. 'Maybe someone *will* come,' he replied. 'But we don't want to have to start building shelters in the dark.'

Rick smiled. 'I was right,' he said. 'I am in good hands. I think I'll get a bit more sleep.'

Suddenly there was a yell from the shore. 'I've got one,' called Andy triumphantly. 'Come and see.' He followed Priya's example and tapped the fish's head sharply on a rock.

Two hours later they had seven fish lined up on the bank. None of them had been as easy to catch as Abby's. When Jay's turn finally came, he had waited over an hour before the rod twitched in his hands. They had seen the helicopter twice more in the distance to the north, but although they had fed the fire with green wood and leafy branches and reeds so that a column of smoke rose constantly into the air, there was still no sign of rescue.

Connor looked down at the line of silver fish. He took out his knife and handed it to Priya. 'Why don't you do it?' he said. 'You were easily the best at it the other day, and we don't want to waste anything.'

They all watched in admiration as Priya expertly ran the keen blade of Connor's knife along the belly of each fish and scraped the innards into the hole that he had dug. Connor took each fish from her and spitted it on a green stick that he had prepared. He had carefully stripped the bark and sharpened both ends like a skewer.

'OK,' said Toby, 'Let's get cooking.'

He and Jay had found two large fallen branches in the wood and had brought them back, ready to place on either side of the fire. They had let the flames die down and the fire was now a bed of glowing embers.

'Perfect,' said Connor as he laid the sticks carefully across the two logs.

They squatted around the fire as the fish began to hiss and spit in the heat. A delicious smell wafted into the air – sizzling fish mingled with wood smoke. Minutes later they were all pulling the steaming, tender flesh from the bones.

'I don't know about you lot,' Abby said, licking her fingers, 'but this is the most delicious fish I've ever eaten.'

'Actually,' said Jay, 'I reckon it might be the most delicious *meal* I've ever eaten.'

'But what about Rick?' asked Priya quietly. 'He didn't eat any of his.'

Rick had woken briefly, and even smiled when he saw the fish, but then he'd closed his eyes again.

'I think it's OK for him to sleep,' Connor said. 'But we do have to watch him in case he's sick or his headache gets worse. It's seven o'clock now – it'll start getting dark at about nine. I think we should try and get some sleep then and be up as soon as it's light. They're much more likely to find us then. But we should make sure there's always someone awake to check on Rick and keep the fire going.'

They all nodded their agreement. 'OK, then,' Connor continued. 'Why don't we tell stories? It's a shame we haven't got any marshmallows to toast.'

'Well, as it happens,' said Toby, 'I did put a bag in. They don't weigh much,' he added as they all stared at him, open-mouthed. 'I'll go and get them, shall I?'

'Toby!' Abby exclaimed when he returned with the marshmallows. 'You are a total genius!'

He blushed as he speared one on a stick and handed it to her. 'It'll be a bit fishy,' he said, 'but I bet it'll still taste good.'

Toby was in the middle of a dream when he woke with a start, certain that something was wrong. It took him a long moment to remember where he was, but then it all came back to him in a rush – the long nightmare journey down the river; the terrifying chaos of the churning water below the weir. But it wasn't this that had woken him. It was something else.

He heaved himself upright, trying not to disturb Jay, who was asleep beside him. They had all sat by the fire telling stories and jokes until the first stars appeared in the deepening blue-green sky. Now the night was black overhead and the only light came from the dim glow of the fire. The sound of the swollen river was still loud as it rushed past on either side of the island. It looked like everyone had gone to sleep . . . *Everyone!*

Someone should be awake! Someone should be standing guard, but they weren't. And the fire wasn't just low, it was nearly out. Toby moved towards it, his heart thumping, and saw Andy lying beside it, fast asleep. It must have been his turn to take watch. Well, there was no harm done. He could take over from Andy himself, but first there was Rick to check on. He felt in his pocket, found his head torch and switched it on, careful not to shine it directly into Rick's shelter and wake him.

He stood there, horrified. Rick was gone.

For a moment Toby couldn't believe his eyes. He looked right into the shelter, but it was empty. He ran over to Connor, who was turning uneasily in his sleep. 'Connor!' he said loudly. 'Wake up! Rick's gone!'

Connor sat up and blinked, dazzled by the torch. 'Sorry,' said Toby, pointing it at the ground. 'We have to wake everyone. Rick isn't there. He must have woken up and wandered off.'

Connor leaped to his feet. Quickly they roused

the others and Toby explained what had happened.

'I'm sorry . . .' Andy was mortified. 'I didn't mean to go to sleep.'

'It's OK,' said Connor. 'We're all exhausted. It could have happened to any of us. What matters now is to find Rick quickly. It's an island, remember. He can't have gone far. We'll head for the northern end, then we can spread out and search. Put your head torches on. It'll be fine as long as we make sure we can always see the torches of the people on either side of us. Are you all ready?'

Toby could sense that they were all thinking the same terrible thought. What if Rick had stumbled into that river? He wouldn't have a chance. His hands felt clammy and his heart was beating fast as they moved along the shore to the end of the island and turned to begin the search. It was hard, moving through the shadowy trees. Unseen branches caught at him and leaves brushed against his face. The sound of the river faded a little as they moved into the woods, but it was always there. As they moved forward, they all called Rick's name, shouting even louder as they approached the southern end of the island. But there was no sign of him anywhere.

'We could easily have missed him in the darkness,' Andy said miserably. 'He probably went back to sleep. It's hopeless – and it's all my fault.'

They were standing at the very tip of the island; they could sense the size and power of the river all around them.

'We'll search again,' Connor decided.

'Wait,' said Toby as they started to move. 'We were making a lot of noise on the way down. Let's go twenty paces forward, all call Rick's name, then stop and listen.'

'Good,' agreed Connor. 'Let's do it.'

They set off once more, this time moving a short distance through the trees, then stopping, calling and listening. It was Priya's sharp ears that heard the sound. 'Listen!' she called. 'I'm sure I heard something.'

They all stopped and then moved with difficulty through the undergrowth to join her.

'What did you hear?' Connor asked urgently. 'Where was it?'

'It's hard to tell,' Priya replied. 'The river is so loud, but I'm sure I heard someone calling somewhere over there.' She gestured towards the river.

Suddenly the sound came again, a low moan, and this time they all heard it.

Toby turned his head in the direction of the sound and something flashed in the beam of his head torch. 'There!' he said. 'It's him, I'm sure it is!'

He struggled through nettles and trailing brambles, trying desperately to keep his torch focused on the place where he had seen the flash of reflected light. 'Rick?' he called. 'Are you there?' He paused. Then, just as he was about to give up, he heard Rick's voice.

'Toby? Is that you?'

Toby turned towards the sound, and his torch picked out Rick's pale face and bandaged head. He was lying full length on the ground, his legs ensnared in brambles. His hand went up to shield his eyes from the light, and the glass of his wristwatch flashed. That must have been what Toby had seen.

'Are you OK?' Toby asked him. 'Hey, everyone, I've found him. Over here!'

'I'll be fine,' said Rick weakly as the other Tigers joined them and looked anxiously down at him, 'just as soon as you all shine those torches somewhere else!'

CHAPTER 16

'What happened?' asked Connor as he helped Rick to sit up, and Toby set to work cutting the bramble stems away from his legs. 'Are you all right?'

'You know what?' replied Rick. 'I have absolutely no idea how I got here. I thought I was dreaming, but I must have been sleepwalking. It's this bump on my head. I was having a nightmare and I was all tangled up in some kind of rope and I couldn't get out. Then I woke up, and everything was dark, and I really was trapped. I can't believe it was only brambles.'

'Do you think you can walk?' asked Connor anxiously. 'Me and Andy will help you.'

'I'll try. Here, give me your arm.'

With the help of the two boys, Rick got unsteadily to his feet and they began to walk back towards the camp. 'I can't tell you how glad I was to hear your voices,' he said. 'And the funny thing is, I feel better now. My headache seems to have gone.'

'You know what?' Priya said suddenly. 'I think it's getting light. I can actually see where I'm going.'

Sure enough, the sky ahead of them was no longer black. Connor could make out the outlines of the trees against the grey sky. Above their heads, a bird began to sing.

They pushed on more quickly, with Connor and Andy supporting Rick. When they reached the camp, Connor took out his knife and quickly began stripping shavings from a dry stick. As soon as he had enough, he bent down and stirred up the ash in the fireplace, revealing a handful of glowing embers. He threw the shavings on top and blew on them. A small bright flame sprang up almost immediately, and Connor piled on bigger and bigger twigs until the fire was crackling merrily and giving off real heat.

Andy and Abby helped Rick back to his

shelter. 'How are you feeling?' Connor asked him. 'Is there anything we can do?'

'You've done a lot,' Rick told him wearily. 'We just have to hope that they find us soon. I need to rest now.' He lay down and closed his eyes.

Connor shivered and turned to meet the anxious eyes of the other Tigers.

'There must be *something* we can do,' said Andy.

'It's properly light now,' Abby pointed out. 'And listen . . .'

Behind them, Rick muttered in his sleep and rolled over. More birds began to sing. And then the other Tigers heard it too – the distant throb of a helicopter. It grew a little louder, and then faded away.

'There *is* something we can do,' Toby said suddenly. 'Let's try to get their attention. Gather up loads of grass and leaves. Anything that'll make smoke.'

'We tried that yesterday,' Abby said. 'Nobody came.'

'We'll make smoke signals this time. Take

down one of the shelters – we can use the tarp. Have you noticed – the wind has died down. The smoke will go straight up.'

'Have you been watching old black-and-white western movies?' asked Andy. 'This isn't the wild west.'

'There might be other fires,' Toby insisted. 'We have to make sure they know it's us. We can use the international distress signal. Six puffs of smoke, then a gap. They'll see it from miles away. We have to *try* it. What have we got to lose?'

'Toby's right,' Connor said. 'Come on, everyone. Old nettle stalks are good, and there are loads of dead leaves. We'll make a big pile and then we'll start.'

'I'll stay here and build up the fire,' Toby said.

Connor and the others moved off into the wood, gathering armfuls of material for the fire. Before long they had made a huge pile. Toby had already encouraged the fire into an enormous blaze, heaping the biggest logs he could find on the top. 'I think that'll be enough,' he said finally. 'Let's start making signals.'

'What do we do?' asked Priya.

'We chuck loads of that stuff on top of the fire,' Toby said, 'and then we put the tarp over the top. We'll have to make sure the fire doesn't break out again or it'll melt the tarp.'

'Are you sure this is going to work?' Andy looked doubtful.

'Just watch the fire,' Toby said. 'We'll need one of us on each corner of the tarp. You and Abby take care of the fire. OK, here we go.'

They flung armfuls of damp grass and leaves onto the fire and the flames instantly disappeared. A cloud of choking smoke swirled around them, making their eyes sting and catching in their throats.

'Quick,' yelled Toby. 'Get the tarp on top.'

Connor grabbed his corner. Toby was beside him, and on the opposite side Priya and Jay were blinking and coughing as the smoke blew into their faces. They brought the tarp down over the fire and the air cleared. Smoke oozed from under the edges of the plastic. 'One, two, three . . . GO!' yelled Toby.

They lifted the tarp and a huge grey-black cloud rose up through the trees. 'Get it back on!' Toby ordered. 'Don't stand there watching it . . .'

A few moments later they were smothering the smoke for the sixth time. 'Now we wait,' he said. 'About a minute I should think . . .'

'Just lift the edge,' Abby said. 'We need to get more green stuff under there.'

As Toby lifted his corner, Connor saw small flames licking along the edge of the grass. Abby and Andy damped them down quickly with another load of damp leaves.

'OK,' said Toby. 'Let's do it again.'

For more than an hour they kept up the signals, taking it in turns to feed the fire and manage the signalling. They soon realized that one of the fire-tenders would have to collect more green stuff while the other took care of the fire, and as time went by, they had to race further and further into the wood to find supplies.

'I can't keep this up much longer,' gasped Jay, staggering back into the clearing with a huge armful of nettles. 'My hands are stinging so much I can't even feel the new stings.'

'That's six . . .' Connor lowered the tarp and stretched his aching back. 'Maybe we should take a break.'

'No!' cried Jay. 'Listen!'

It was the unmistakable sound of a helicopter. Connor dragged the tarp off the fire, allowing the column of smoke to rise straight up again. Immediately they all ran down to the shore and looked up to see the orange helicopter flying directly towards them, low over the flooded river.

It came in fast. Connor dashed closer to the river and stood with his arms in the shape of a Y, but the helicopter flew straight over their heads, and then they heard the sound fade away upstream.

'It's pointless, isn't it?' said Abby despondently. 'We might as well just let the fire burn.'

'No,' Toby insisted doggedly. 'They *must* have seen us. Let's keep signalling to make quite sure. Connor gave the sign that we need rescuing. Someone will come.'

Wearily they returned to their task. Connor cast an anxious glance at Rick, but his condition didn't seem to have changed. They had only sent up two more clouds of smoke when Connor heard the sound of an engine. 'Stop!' he said. 'I think it's—'

'It's a boat!' screamed Priya. 'Quick, everyone! We're going to be rescued!'

Looking through the trees, Connor saw an orange RIB powering down the river towards the island. Orange-clad figures stood up in it, pointing towards them. He suddenly felt weak and dizzy, and the world started to swim in front of his eyes.

The rest of the Tigers came to join him by the river, and he heard Rick calling weakly to him.

'Hey, Connor, are you OK? Is that a boat I can hear?'

Connor took a deep breath. 'Yes,' he said. 'It's going to be OK, Rick. We're all going to be safe.'

He heard the roar of the boat's engine change to a deep, slow throb – and then voices coming through the trees. He walked slowly towards the sound and saw a burly man in an orange survival suit wading ashore.

The stranger introduced himself. 'I'm Kevin – I need to know who *you* are. I'm hoping you're Scouts from the Matfield Group.'

'We are,' confirmed Connor. 'We—'

'There should be six of you, right? And your leader. Where's he?'

'He's hurt,' Connor said as Kevin counted them – and then counted them again before turning and calling to the boat, 'They're all here. You can call in that the kids are OK. Brian, you'd best come ashore. They say their leader's injured.'

Brian was a tall thin man with a rucksack full of medical supplies. He followed the Tigers back to the clearing, where Rick had pulled himself up into a sitting position. Brian undid the bandage and inspected his head wound, which was now surrounded by an evil-looking yellow bruise spreading down the side of his face. As he worked, the Tigers told him what had happened.

Connor looked up and saw an expression of blank astonishment and disbelief on Kevin's face.

'You came through that weir?' he said. 'All of you, on a log raft? That's the most amazing thing I've ever heard. We never dreamed you'd made it all the way down here. There's so much flooded farmland back up river that the search has been concentrated there.'

'We thought it must have been something like that,' Abby said.

'Aye, well, they found one of your kayaks up there. There's been plenty of people looking for you.'

Connor suddenly thought of their parents. 'They'll tell them, won't they?' he asked. 'I mean, they'll tell all the people who're worried about us?'

'Already done,' said Kevin. 'OK, looks like we're ready to go.'

'Not quite.' Brian had been re-bandaging Rick's head. 'We'll need a stretcher. No point in taking any chances, even after all the crazy stuff you've been doing.'

'We can pack up our stuff then,' said Toby.

'You don't need to do that,' Kevin told him.

'Someone will come back for your kayaks.'

Toby shook his head. 'We can do it while they're getting Rick ready. We'd rather leave this island as we found it. Right, everyone?'

There was a chorus of agreement from the Tigers, and while Kevin shook his head in surprise, they set about extinguishing the fire and packing up their gear. By the time Rick was settled on the stretcher there was only a patch of trampled grass to show where the Scout camp had been.

'I've always wanted to go on one of these,' said Andy as they took their places on the RIB.

'Why do they call it that?' asked Jay, fastening his seat belt.

'Rigid Inflatable Boat,' said Toby.

'It's an inshore lifeboat,' Martin, the skipper, told them. 'We brought it upstream to help with the search. Normally we're out at sea.'

'Well, we're glad you were here,' said Andy, taking out his camera and clicking the shutter. 'Just one left,' he said, winding the film on. 'I think I'll save it for when we're back on dry land.'

'That won't be long.' Kevin grinned as Martin put the engine in gear and the boat gathered speed, leaving a wide trail of churning white water in its wake.

Five minutes later the boat drew up alongside a concrete slip at the edge of a small town. The crew helped the weary Tigers out of the boat. As they walked up the ridged concrete of the slipway, Connor saw a waiting ambulance and heard a voice yelling his name. He looked up and saw Julie, her face white beneath her tan, eyes red-rimmed from lack of sleep. She hugged every one of them before she spoke.

'I've spoken to your parents,' she said. 'They know you're safe. We're going to take you to hospital and get you checked over. You especially, Toby. You look like you've been in a battle with wild animals. Then, if you really are OK, we'll take you to a hotel.'

Toby looked down at himself. The plaster had come off the cut in his leg and his clothes were damp and ragged and torn by the frantic races through the woods. The others didn't look much better. Their faces were blackened by smoke from the fire, and Connor's hair was full of leaves and twigs.

'You see what I mean?' Julie's face finally relaxed into a smile.

'Hi, Julie,' said Rick as he was carried past on his stretcher. 'Some leader, huh?'

Julie reached out and gave his hand a squeeze.

Rick smiled at her. 'I should have known better than to go on an expedition with this lot . . . But you know what? I'm very glad I did.'

CHAPTER 17

'I think maybe I could eat just one more sausage,' said Toby, helping himself from the large platter in the middle of the table.

'Me too,' said a very clean-looking Connor. 'And I could probably manage some more of that bacon too.'

The Tigers were sitting in the hotel's dining room. The doctors at the hospital had checked them over thoroughly and decided that there was nothing wrong with them that sleep and food wouldn't cure. The long window opposite looked out over the wide, glittering expanse of the flooded river. The far bank seemed a very long way off. They had all eaten one normal breakfast and now, to the astonishment of the other diners in the restaurant, they were well on their way through a second.

'Mmmm,' said Priya. 'I think I'll have a couple of slices of toast and jam.' Alone among the Tigers she had managed to keep her clothes in perfect condition and still looked as if she had stepped straight out of the pages of a fashion magazine – even though she was wearing a perfectly ordinary T-shirt and combat trousers.

But that wasn't right, Toby realized suddenly as he swallowed the last of his sausage. There were a couple of small tears in her T-shirt, and one of her trouser pockets was badly ripped.

Priya saw him looking at her and grinned. 'You had a bath, then, Toby? I thought you might have had enough of water. Every time we go anywhere you fall in.'

'It was great,' Toby said, and the others nodded their agreement. The bath had been deep and hot and Toby had stayed in until his skin had turned wrinkly. Now, he turned back to his breakfast and spread butter on a slice of toast, followed by a thick layer of jam.

'Honestly, Toby,' laughed Julie. 'Anyone would think you hadn't eaten for a week. It's only been a couple of days, and you told me you had a delicious fish supper last night.'

'*One* little fish,' he corrected.

'And we wouldn't have had that if it hadn't been for Toby,' said Andy. 'I'm pretty sure I got a shot of him with his fish. I can't wait to get that film developed.'

Over breakfast they had told Julie every detail of their journey down the flooded river. She had already heard about Rick's accident, because Connor had described it to the paramedics, with all the other Tigers chipping in with things they remembered. The paramedics had asked them lots of questions about Rick's behaviour afterwards.

'He will be all right, won't he?' Connor had asked as they were about to get in the ambulance and drive off. 'I mean, we didn't do anything to make it worse.'

The paramedic had smiled at that and put a hand on Connor's shoulder. 'You did everything you possibly could,' he'd said. 'You got him to safety, didn't you?'

Toby realized he'd been miles away. He stared down at the piece of toast in his hand and there seemed to be two of them. He blinked hard and the two pieces of toast were one again. Suddenly he saw that the others were laughing, and Julie was saying something.

'You're falling asleep, Toby. Your eyes keep closing.'

'Sorry,' he said. 'I don't know what's wrong with me.' He yawned hugely and then realized that all the others were yawning too.

'Bed,' said Julie. 'All of you, right now. Off you go.'

Connor woke up to the dazzle of brilliant sunlight flooding in through a window, and for a moment had no idea where he was. Then he saw his dad standing at the end of his bed and everything came back to him in a rush. He sat up and was astonished to see his mum sitting beside him. 'Mum? What are you doing here?'

'What do you think we're doing?' said his sister, Ellie. 'We came to wake you up. You would have slept all day if I hadn't drawn back those curtains.'

Connor realized that he'd been so tired he hadn't even got into bed; he'd just collapsed on top in his clothes. He stood up and hugged his mum. She held him very tightly, and when she let him go Connor saw that she'd been crying.

Ellie came over to him and hugged him too. 'You're a pain in the neck, little brother,' she said, and Connor saw that even she had tears in her eyes.

'I'm sorry,' he said. 'There wasn't anything we could do about it. It just happened.'

'That's not true.' Connor's dad was smiling at him. 'You did plenty. I'm proud of you, Connor. We all are.'

Connor felt himself flushing. His eyes were stinging embarrassingly.

'We *are* proud of you,' said his mum, 'but in future, if you can possibly manage it, I'd rather not have all the worry.'

Connor rubbed his eyes. 'What about Rick?' he asked. 'Have you heard anything?'

'He's going to be fine, thanks to you,' Dr Sutcliff told him. 'But they're keeping him in hospital overnight to make sure.'

'Can we go and see him?'

'Sure. But right now I think you've got an appointment to keep downstairs.'

'An appointment? What do you mean? And where's Andy?'

Connor had been sharing the room with Andy and he remembered his friend collapsing on the other bed. But there was no sign of him now.

'He's downstairs,' said Mrs Sutcliff. 'So are the rest of them. We waited an hour before Ellie decided to wake you up.'

'But I should be there,' Connor said.

'Not just yet.' His dad was holding something. 'I think you should put this on before you go down.'

'My uniform!'

'We'll wait outside,' Dr Sutcliff said. 'You should hurry.'

Connor put on the uniform, wondering as he

did so why his dad had to be so mysterious. He didn't have long to wait.

His parents led him along the corridor to the lift and they descended in silence. The followed another corridor, opened a door, and suddenly the air erupted in a blast of yelling and cheering.

Connor stared speechlessly at the room full of Scouts and their parents. Everyone was there – Guy and Sajiv, Kerry and Leroy – all of them, cheering. And there were the Sea Scouts too. Connor saw Sam's face smiling at him, and Max, and Joey, their leader cheering as loud as anyone. Connor knew he had gone bright red and had a stupid grin on his face, but somehow he didn't care.

'OK,' said Julie, when the noise finally died down. 'Now, the hotel have put on a bit of a spread for us next door, although I don't suppose the Tigers will be able to eat a thing, not after the mountain of breakfast they put away.'

'You're kidding, aren't you?' Abby laughed. 'Just show us the way.'

There was laughter, but Julie raised a hand.

'Before we do that, there are a couple of TV crews waiting outside, and several journalists who want to talk to you. You probably haven't seen a TV yet, but I can tell you that Tiger Patrol have been national news. A lot of people were very worried about you. Do you think you can manage to talk to the press?'

'I think maybe it should just be the Patrol Leader and the Assistant Patrol Leader and their parents,' said a tall man in Scout uniform who was sitting behind Julie. 'I'm Simon Carter,' he told them. 'From Scout Association HQ at Gilwell Park. I'll be with you when you're interviewed, and so will your parents, and we'll be telling everyone what an excellent job you did.'

'But it was *all* of us,' Connor said. 'We should *all* go. Everyone did something important. We're a team.'

'Well, OK, then,' replied Simon with a twinkle of satisfaction in his eyes. 'Let's go and tell them just how resourceful Scouts can be!'

He led them through a door and down yet another corridor, and they emerged into a blaze of flash guns. The massive lenses of TV cameras stared at them, lights blinking, and there was a hail of clicking shutters. Voices called out from every direction, but finally the Tigers were seated behind a long table with Simon Carter and Julie, their parents standing behind them.

Connor answered the questions that came his way as well as he could, but afterwards the only thing he remembered about the press conference was Andy.

Simon had just thanked the reporters and was getting to his feet when Andy suddenly produced the little disposable camera that he had carried with him through the entire adventure. 'Do you think someone could take our photo?' he asked. 'I've only got one shot left and it would be great if it was of all of us.'

There was laughter from the crowd, and a suntanned woman in jeans and a sweatshirt stepped forward, pushing her own massive camera round onto her back as she took Andy's from him. 'Cool,' she said. 'I haven't used one of these for a long time. Smile, everyone!'

The shutter clicked and there was a round of applause. 'I'll give you a tip,' the photographer said to Andy. 'The pictures in that camera could be worth a lot of money. Enough to buy you a better camera, that's for sure!'

'That was fun,' said Jay to his mum as they made their way back towards the restaurant. 'But I'm glad it's over.'

'We're going to be on TV!' she said. 'All of us – even you, Harry!' She gave Jay's dad a playful poke.

'Yeah, well, they deserve all the fuss,' Jay's dad commented. 'Best idea I ever had, sending Jay to Scouts.'

'*Your* idea!' exclaimed his mum. 'I don't think so.'

Connor was following behind them, grinning to himself, thinking of the sullen, angry boy who had turned up at Scouts that evening back in September. Jay had definitely not wanted to join, but his quick thinking had saved them when Toby had capsized. Priya had joined at the same time, and there she was with her parents, still looking as cool as ever. Looking at her now, he thought, you would never guess that she could paddle a kayak down dangerous rapids with the skill of a veteran.

As they entered the restaurant, they saw that all their friends had already started on the feast laid on by the hotel. Connor saw Sam and Max coming towards him.

'Some people have all the luck.' Sam was smiling at him. 'I'd give anything to have an adventure like that.'

She gazed into Connor's eyes and he found himself feeling unaccountably embarrassed. He looked away and found Abby watching him curiously.

Her mum was with her, and her dad too. He'd flown back from the USA when he'd heard about the floods; he looked nearly as tired as Connor had felt earlier. Abby's eyes were twinkling as she turned to Sam.

'We owe you,' she said to her and Max. 'If we hadn't spent that afternoon on the rapids we'd never have known how to handle those floods.

And Connor would still be upside down in the river if he hadn't watched you two rolling your kayaks.'

'You had to roll it?' exclaimed Sam.

'I didn't have much choice,' replied Connor. 'But I expect Rick would have rescued me.'

There was a pause.

'He'll be OK, won't he?' asked Max.

'That's what they say,' Connor replied. 'We should really—'

He was interrupted by Toby, who joined them with his mum at his side. Like Toby she was small and dark, her black, expensively cut hair falling across her face. She was hanging onto Toby's arm as if she didn't want to let go of him for a moment, and Connor realized that Toby had grown. He was taller than his mum now. When had that happened? he wondered. It occurred to him that they had all grown a lot in the last year – in more ways than one.

'I'd really like to go and see Rick,' Toby said. 'Do you think we can leave yet?'

'Sure,' said Connor. 'I'll go and find Julie.

Andy's over there with his mum and dad.'

'I'll get them,' said Abby. 'See you, Sam, Max.' And she rushed off.

'I'd better go,' Connor said to the Sea Scouts.

'Here,' said Sam suddenly, thrusting a piece of paper into the top pocket of his shirt. 'Keep in touch.' She flushed and turned away to find the rest of her friends.

'I think she likes you,' Max said with a grin. 'Bye, Connor. Like Sam said, keep in touch.'

They exchanged high-fives and Connor, confused and happy, made his way over to find Julie. 'We'd like to go and see Rick now,' he said as the other Tigers and their families joined them. 'Is that OK?'

Julie smiled. 'Of course,' she said. 'We'll go in the minibus. Some of you might have to follow in cars. Come on . . .'

'You have got to be joking,' said the ward manager, a young man with a harassed expression on his thin face. 'Two visitors at a time, that's the rule. Three at a push. There are nineteen of you!

I'm having enough trouble with him as it is. He won't stay in bed. Insists on sitting up in his chair. And then there was the press! It's been a madhouse here.'

'Well, if he's sitting up already,' said Julie, 'couldn't I bring him out here to the day room? It can't do any harm, can it?'

'You're the kids who were with him, aren't you?' said the man. 'I saw you on the TV. Well, I suppose . . .'

'Great!' said Julie. 'Thanks. I'll go and fetch him.'

Moments later a wheelchair emerged from a side room and they saw Rick's face. There were gasps from the parents, and even Connor was shocked. The bruising seemed to have got worse, and Rick's left eye was blackened and swollen nearly shut. The wound in his forehead had been neatly stapled together, and Rick was grinning broadly at them.

'It's not nearly as bad as it looks,' he told them as Julie pushed him into the day room and they all followed him inside. 'They've done all kinds of tests and there's nothing broken. I'm going to be fine, thanks to this lot.'

The Tigers burst out with a chorus of questions, but Rick held up his hand. 'Listen, everyone,' he said, looking past the Scouts to their parents. 'I know you were worried about these guys, and I'm not saying we weren't in danger out there. But we're all back safely, and it's mainly thanks to them. From what I can understand, every single one of them deserves a lot of praise.'

There was a chorus of agreement from the parents. Connor knew his face was going red, but he didn't care, and he felt his dad's hand squeezing his shoulder.

'I've got some news for you too,' Rick continued. 'Just to prove that my brain is still working, I've been adding up Toby and Connor's badges. You probably won't be surprised to hear that they've both qualified for the Chief Scout's Gold Award.'

There was more cheering at this, and Connor and Toby exchanged high-fives with the other

Tigers before the ward manager put his head round the door and asked them to keep the noise down.

'I'm sure the rest of you will get your awards next year,' Rick said. 'You're collecting badges as if there was no tomorrow. But of course, you'll be doing it without Connor and Toby because they'll be leaving to join the Explorer Scouts.'

Connor suddenly felt deflated. In all the excitement he had actually forgotten that this was the Tigers' final expedition together, and he could see that the others had too.

'Don't worry, Connor,' said Priya suddenly. 'We'll make sure that Tiger Patrol just goes on getting better.'

'That's good,' said Julie, smiling, 'because they'll have a lot to live up to. Rick and I have been talking to Simon Carter. He thinks we should put you all forward for the Meritorious Conduct Medal.'

There was another round of cheers that not even the ward manager's reappearance could stop. A couple of patients pushed their way past him into the day room. 'Don't make such a fuss, young man,' said an elderly lady in a flowery dressing gown. 'This is Tiger Patrol. They're famous. We've been watching them on TV! Let us in – we want to see what's going on.'

The ward manager laughed. 'Oh, go on then . . . But you do actually need to rest, Rick,' he told the Scout Leader. 'Five minutes and this lot are leaving.'

'He's right,' Rick said. 'But I want to say one more thing before you all leave. You guys have proved that you can stay calm in the face of the very worst that nature can throw at you. I reckon you've earned your name on this trip. You really *are* the Survival Squad!'

TIPS FOR BUILDING A LOG RAFT Notes from Abby

YOU NEED:

- 5-8 logs about three metres long and 25-30 cm in diameter.
- 2 more logs about 10 cm in diameter that overlap the big ones by about 15 cm at each end. These are the connector logs.
- Plenty of rope!
- Dry dead wood is best, and pine, fir, and poplar are all quite light.

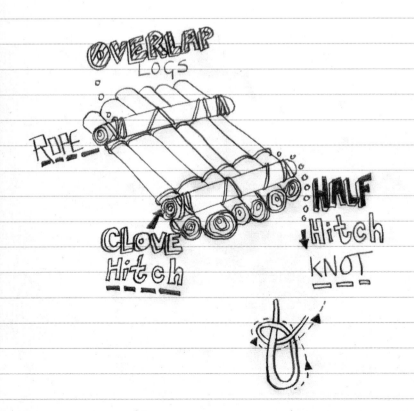

It's a good idea to assemble the raft either in the water or very near it. Even light logs are hard to lift when they're all tied together!

Use a clove hitch to fasten the rope to the connector log, and a square lashing to tie each log on. You need a half hitch after each log, and another clove hitch to finish.

Make sure all your knots and lashings are tight!

Refs: http://www.raftplan.com/lograft.aspx

Scout Handbook: pp144 and 149

MAKING A COOKING FIRE Notes from Connor

Make sure you've collected all the wood you need before you start.

- Grade your wood and store it carefully. Cover it with a plastic sheet if you have one.
- Build the fire carefully. Light the tinder, then add kindling, then larger pieces of wood.
- A good cooking fire needs heat, but no flames or smoke. Put on larger pieces of wood and allow them to burn down to red-hot embers.
- Try to keep one part of the fire always ready for cooking.
- NEVER LEAVE THE FIRE UNATTENDED.
- Always have a safety bucket of water, sand or fine soil, or a pile if you don't have a bucket.

Ref: Scout Handbook
p126

SAFETY STONES

LIFT FROM FLAMES

KINDLING

TIMBER

H2O WATER

Cooking Fire

BIVOUACS   Notes from Toby

Things to remember:

- Small is good.
- Make sure you have insulation underneath you. Ferns and leaves will trap air.
- Use anything you can find. Be prepared to improvise.
- Simple, lean-to shelters are often good. If you have a kayak you can stand it on its side and use it as one wall of a shelter.
- You can use plastic sheets strung between trees.

The aim is to keep warm and dry, and get your bivouac built fast.

Ref: Scout Handbook p199

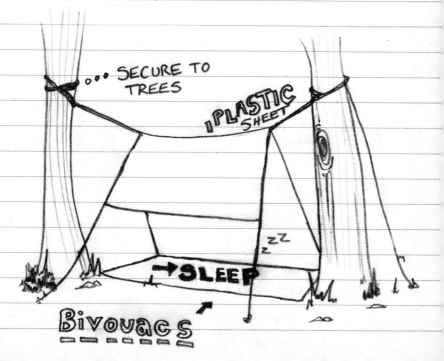

WILD FOOD TO EAT Notes from Priya

What you can find depends on the time of year. Here
are some things you can eat at different seasons:

SPRING
Hawthorn buds
Nettle tips (they make good soup!)

SUMMER
Wild garlic
Fennel
Wood sorrel

AUTUMN
Hazelnuts
Sweet chestnuts

And you can always try to
catch fish!

KNOTS USED IN THIS ADVENTURE   Notes from Jay

Clove hitch: This is often used to begin other hitches and lashings. We used it for the log rafts.

Round turn and two half hitches: A simple hitch used to attach a rope to a spar, post or tree. Toby used it to attach line to a fishing rod on the island.

Sheet bend: Toby used this to fasten a rope to the painter of my (Connor's) kayak when we rescued Rick on the island. It is used to fasten two ropes of different thicknesses together.

Clinch knot: Toby used this to fasten a hook to the fishing line.

Refs: For the first three see Scout Handbook pp 143-145

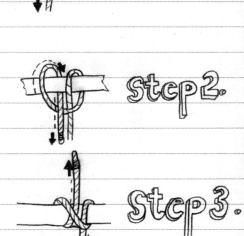

THE INTERNATIONAL DISTRESS SIGNAL Notes from Andy

In the UK and the European Alps the distress signal is based on groups of six. Everywhere else they use groups of three, but the main thing is to do a pattern of three or six and then repeat it once a minute.

The signal can be sounds, or it can be visual. So it could be blasts on a whistle or a horn, or shouts, or it could be flashes of light or you could wave clothing, or even signal with smoke.

The answer to the signal is three flashes, or blasts.

If a helicopter is in sight, the signal for needing help is to make a Y shape with your arms.

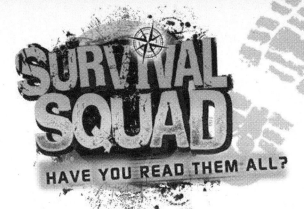

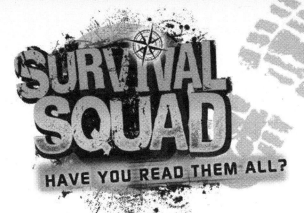

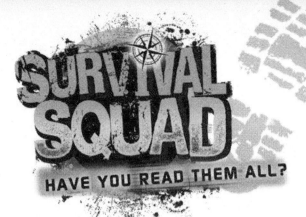

HAVE YOU READ THEM ALL?

THE THRILLING THIRD INSTALMENT IN THE
SURVIVAL SQUAD SERIES!

FROM SNOW RESCUES TO MIDNIGHT BIKE RIDES
AND MYSTERY, SURVIVAL SQUAD ARE
ALWAYS UP FOR A CHALLENGE.